Mary's Adventures

Mary's Adventures

A Kinky Companions Novella

Alex Markson

This paperback edition 2020

First published by Parignon Press 2019

Copyright © Alex Markson 2019

Alex Markson asserts the moral right to be identified as the author of this work in accordance with the Copyright, Designs and Patents Act 1988

ISBN: 979 8 61 726326 0

Prologue

An old tart.

That's what Sally had called me after my confession to her. It was said in jest; at least, I think it was. She'd taken it well and it hadn't affected our relationship. But it wasn't something I was proud of. It was a long time ago, and I'd not really thought about it for years.

Our conversation had made me think back to those times. When I'd been young and carefree; and a bit ... loose. That word always made me smile. I'd told Sally that's what her mother – my sister – would probably have called me; though never to my face. Catherine was too polite for that. Or should that be repressed? I wasn't sure then, and I'm not sure now, all these years later.

Catherine is long gone, unfortunately, and I don't think I ever really knew her. We weren't close. She looked out for me, but I was five years younger than her, and we were never close emotionally. We never shared our secrets or desires. I had lots of those, but I'm not sure she did. When she got married at twenty-five, I was twenty, but far more experienced than her.

Looking back, I did benefit from being the younger sister. Our parents were less strict with me than they were with Catherine, and I think she resented that. Although what she wanted to do that she couldn't, I don't know. It was me who went through the wild times: the music, the clothes. The boys. She never showed much interest in any of those things. Until she met Tony.

So, I've spent some time recently thinking back to those years; my formative years. A few memories have made me wince, but most have been happy memories of good times. Some, very good times. I'm not going to share those memories with Sally. But I thought I might share a few with you. If you'd like to hear them.

***

I grew up in the swinging sixties, but I was too young for the decade to have any lasting effect on me. It passed my parents by completely. I was really a child of the seventies and they left an indelible mark on me. I guess your teenage years always do. Fleeting friendships, as you learn how to distinguish the genuine from the convenient. Changing fads in clothes, music and TV programmes.

Looking back, these things seemed to change more quickly in the seventies than at any time since. But that may just be because it was my decade. Every year produced a completely new range of music and fashion. Prog rock, through glam rock, punk, post-punk, and the coming of the new romantics.

All these spawned their own tribal followings and I dabbled in most of them at one time or another. Some very briefly. And alongside these new kids on the block, there was still room for the more traditional genres. Whilst kids in the sixties had to choose between being mods or rockers, or perhaps between the

Beatles or the Stones, we had so many options, we were able to try them all.

When I was ten or eleven, it was David Cassidy; not the Osmonds. Unless I was talking to Julie Williams, who I wanted to be best friends with for a while. She was an Osmonds junky, but the David poster on my bedroom wall gave me away when she finally visited my home one day after school.

My first real love was Roxy Music; well, Bryan Ferry. I remember seeing him on Top of the Pops, and even though I was only twelve or thirteen, I could see how stylish and cool he was. I also saw how many boys tried to copy his mannerisms; all failing dismally. There wasn't anyone like him; never has been.

Then punk came along. I liked it because my parents hated it; like most kids, I suspect. Because let's be honest, a lot of the music was crap. It was the attitude which attracted us. Anti-establishment, anarchic, political, and authentic. The summer of 1976 is the time most people associate with the height of punk. It was for me. The Sex Pistols, The Ramones, The Clash, The Damned. They were all riding high, and I was engrossed in the culture.

I wore some awful clothes but loved them at the time. Getting stared at in the street was something new for me; scary at times, but it also sparked something. I liked being the centre of attention. My parents hated it, but they indulged me. 'She'll grow out of it', I heard them say.

But something else was occupying my thoughts that summer too; sex.

Chapter 1 – The First

Like all of us, I'd been aware of my own body since I was young. I can't remember when I first became aware of sex, as such. But the rather perfunctory lessons we had at school gave names to a few things, and then the playground took over. You know how it is; you'll believe anything you're told for a while. Until someone else tells you the exact opposite; then you believe that.

We didn't know much at all, really, but what we lacked in knowledge, we made up for in imagination. How to get pregnant; how not to get pregnant. And that awful day you suddenly realised that your parents must have done this act, otherwise you wouldn't be here. Twice if you had a sibling.

You have to remember; this was well before the internet. We couldn't just look stuff up. Although the internet seems to have just as much rubbish as our school playground did. I tried the library, but the few books they had on the subject were very technical; not at all interesting for a teenager.

Like most of us, my knowledge came from exploring my own body. And those experiments had left me a little confused, but aware that this was a thing I was looking forward to. So, I was expecting my first time to be a highlight of my young life.

It was punk that brought it about. I hung around with a disparate group of kids; all into punk culture. Some were hardcore; anarchic, dropouts, squatting in derelict buildings. I never did that, but for a time, I lived it every day. As did David Skelton.

I'd known him at school, but we hadn't been friends. He'd been a bit of a nerd, but something had happened in his family and he'd dropped out. Now, we found ourselves in the same gang and got to know each other. I liked him. Some of the boys in the group were very pushy when it came to the girls. This was the stone age of sexism, remember. But David wasn't. Looking back, I guess he was very shy, but I didn't see that at the time.

After a while, the group seemed to acknowledge that David and I were an item, so they left us to it. At that point, nothing had happened, but it did mean that the other boys left me alone, which took the pressure off. We met up most weekends, went to gigs and any pub we could get into. David and I had a few kisses, but that was about it. Until the weekend my parents went away.

The gang met up on Saturday afternoon in the town centre and wandered around for a while. We were going to a gig in the evening, so we wasted time sitting around, getting frowned at by all the afternoon shoppers. We had a few drinks in our usual pub, then moved on to the venue. Sweaty, smelly, raucous, occasionally violent. A typical punk gig. Afterwards, we milled around outside, while the various groups cautiously mingled.

"Wanna come home with me, Dave?" I asked.

"Yeah, if you like. Won't your folks object?"

"No. They're away."

"Oh."

We walked along, both quiet. Both thinking our own thoughts. We'd never been alone in private before, so I guess we were both wondering what lay in store. I knew what I wanted; did he? When we got home, I put a Damned album on, and we danced about; well I guess that's what you'd call our arrhythmic jumping. I noticed that he was surreptitiously looking at me a lot; a good sign.

I raided the rather meagre drinks cabinet my parents kept, and we enjoyed ourselves for a while. When the record finished, we flopped down on the sofa to recover. It slowly dawned on me that I was going to have to make the first move. I wasn't sure if that was because he wasn't interested or if he was shy.

Summoning all my courage, I jumped on him and started kissing him. Recovering from his surprise, he started to respond, and we were soon slobbering over each other. Keen but clueless. After a while, we came up for air.

"Ever been with a girl?" I asked.

He looked embarrassed again.

"Uh, no. You?"

"With a girl?"

He went red.

"No. With a boy?"

"No."

We fell silent again.

"Want to?" I finally asked.

"Yeah."

Now we were taking a leap into the unknown. We both knew the technicalities; well, I did. I guess he did as well. But was that enough? We started kissing again, more slowly this time. We were both up for it. I knew the signs well enough in myself. I had that tingle between my legs, and I could feel his dick poking into my thigh as I lay over him. It was the first time I'd come into contact with a real erection. I was eager to get closer.

His courage grew, and he started to run his hands over my body. I enjoyed his touch and kissed him to encourage his exploration. His hand went down to my waist, and slipped under my t-shirt, touching my skin. I flinched at this first contact. He paused, but I smiled, and he carried on, running his hand up until he found my bra.

I reached down, and lifting the hem, pulled my t-shirt off. He stared briefly at my cleavage, before running his hand over it, pushing his fingers down into the bra until he found my nipple. Roughly squeezing it, he rubbed it between his fingers and tried to pull it up out of the bra. But I wasn't a big girl, so it only just popped out. I reached around and undid the fastener and took it off.

He was now staring at my breasts and, looking down, I could now clearly see the bulge in his trousers. Neither of us had said anything while this was going on. I think it was a mixture of anticipation, shyness, and not wanting to say the wrong thing. He now had both hands on my breasts, rubbing and feeling them. My nipples were hard, and he seemed to be enjoying them. The heat between my legs had increased, and I was eager to get my hands on his dick.

I pulled him forward and lifted his t-shirt off. Reaching down, I undid the buttons on his jeans and slipped my hand into them, finally feeling his dick through his briefs. He jumped as I did so. I'd had enough dithering, so got off the sofa, and stood in front of him. Undoing my jeans, I pushed them down and took them off, conscious of his gaze. I grabbed the end of his jeans and started to pull them down his legs. He had to wriggle a bit, but they finally came off. Both of us now just in our pants.

I climbed back on the sofa, and straddled him, my pussy finally resting on his dick, albeit with two layers of material between them. We kissed again, and he put his hands on my back and slowly let them drop down until they reached my bum. I was slowly grinding myself on him; an action that we both seemed to be enjoying.

His hands slid inside my pants, and he squeezed my bum a few times. His breathing seemed to get louder. I let my hand go down to his briefs and pushed it under the waistband. For the first time, I felt a real dick. He took a sharp breath as I circled it with my fingers.

He now got bolder and moved his hands around to my front. Slipping one down, he reached my pussy. This time it was my turn to take a sharp breath, as a hand other than my own touched my sex. He rubbed his hand up and down over my pussy; not knowing what he was supposed to do. I moved off him and, grabbing his briefs, pulled them down as he lifted himself up.

I looked down and stared at his dick. I'm not sure what I expected, but it was fascinating. Hard and veiny with a purple head. His balls were tight against the base. I reached down and started exploring it. Running my fingers up and down, and over his balls. Grabbing it, and encasing it, rubbing up and down.

He was groaning, his hand vigorously, but inexpertly, rubbing up and down inside my pants. It still felt good, though. Finally, I was here. One hand stroking an erect dick, while its owner was stroking my pussy.

I got off him again and quickly took my pants off. Now we were both naked. I pushed him down onto the sofa and lay down on top of him, and we resumed our fumbling. Me playing with his dick, him fingering my pussy. In my own playing, it took me quite some time to orgasm, but I wasn't sure what would happen with a partner. At this point, I was more interested in his dick. I stroked and caressed it, watching his reactions. He'd given up trying to do anything to me; he still had one hand between my legs, but it lay motionless.

I used both hands now. Holding his balls while I ran the other up and down his shaft. It felt hot and pliant, with the veins engorged; his balls tight. The tip covered in his pre-cum. I ran a finger over the head, spreading this liquid around, eliciting more urgent moans from him.

"Wanna do it?"

"Yeah." He'd always been a man of few words.

"I've got a condom."

I got off him and went to my bag. I may not have known much about what I was doing, but I'd known one or two girls who got pregnant at my age, and I was sure I didn't want that to happen. So, I'd prepared. Summoning up my courage; going into a chemist in the next town and buying some condoms. I'd even practised putting one on two of my own fingers.

I took one out of my bag. "Have you tried putting one on?" I asked him.

"No."

"Well, this could be fun."

We both smiled nervously, and I took it out of the packet and passed it to him. He took it in his hand, and I returned to stroking his dick. He looked at the condom. As I cupped his balls and held his dick straight, he placed the condom over the head and attempted to roll it down. He was breathing heavily; nerves, I guessed.

"Other way up," I offered.

"Oh. Right." He turned it over.

Just as he did so, I felt his dick twitch sharply, and cum shot out in an arc and landed on my breasts. Another shot followed, along with some grunts from him, and then a few smaller ones.

9

Now less vigorous, his cum now covered his dick and my hands. After momentary surprise, I watched all this with a mixture of disappointment and fascination.

Silence fell. I could hear David's breathing returning to normal. I looked at him, but he wouldn't meet my eye.

"I ... I'm sorry," he managed. "I couldn't help it."

"It's OK," I replied. "I'll get some tissues."

I went to the bathroom, and after washing my hands, took the box of tissues back to the living room. I watched as he cleaned himself up; still unable to look me in the eye.

"I'm sorry," he said again.

"David, don't worry. This was the first time for both of us. Can you do it again?"

He looked at me for the first time.

"Well, probably. I can normally come more than once in an evening."

Realising what he had admitted, he blushed slightly, and I laughed. It broke the ice a bit, and he smiled in return.

"Good, then we'll try again later."

We did. And this time we actually did it. Both less nervous; both a bit more relaxed. It wasn't exactly earth-shattering; at least not for me. Enjoyable, but I didn't reach orgasm. Not until after he'd had left, anyway.

David and I continued to see each other for a while, and we did learn a few things. At least I showed him what I needed him to do for me. But we were never in love, and after a few months we split up. But you always remember your first time, don't you?

Chapter 2 – The Teacher

I quickly realised that I loved sex. But there was a bit more to it than that. I also loved playing the game. I wasn't exactly beautiful by conventional standards, but I had something that attracted the boys. At the time, I couldn't really identify what it was, but I was confident, flirty and loved showing off. And I gave as good as I got. If a boy I wasn't interested in went too far, he soon knew it.

After David and I split up, I spent the next year playing the field. Every weekend saw me dressed up, and out on the town. But that town was small. Small enough to move around the various pubs and clubs easily, but small enough to ensure that what you got up to was known by everyone the following week. Thankfully, I was at college a few miles away, in a much larger town, and I'd found a good friend there; Paula.

We had gelled almost instantly, and the two of us had similar views on a lot of things. Including boys and sex. So, every Saturday night, we went out looking for both and nearly always found them. We were choosy though, and here, Paula and I differed. She always went for the strong, macho type. The leader of any group. I'd soon found that they were trophy hunters; only wanting to brag about their conquests. Normally, I looked for another member of the group.

Most groups of lads seemed to have the same make-up. A leader, sometimes two. A couple of fawning followers, and a few hangers-on who were merely tolerated, often for their financial input to the drinks bill. Then there would be the one I would look for.

Obviously, a full member of the gang, but slightly apart. Not showy, not fawning, but certain of his right to be there. I found that they were the ideal target and homed in on them. Most Saturday nights ended up with sex in a variety of unsuitable places. In the park, in the graveyard, in a car. Or if you were lucky, and the guy shared a flat with his mates, a proper bed.

I was by now spending a lot of time at Paula's parents. It made going to college much easier, and it was certainly more convenient at the weekends. They were hippies, left over from the previous decade. Very laid back and friendly. They lived in a large, ramshackle house, which seemed to have an ever-changing number of lodgers and visitors. One more – me – went largely unnoticed.

I still remember the ever-present smell of weed hanging over the house. Paula was able to do whatever she wanted, as long as she let them know she was okay. They were very open about sex and had told Paula all those things that my parents hadn't told me; probably didn't even know themselves.

All this meant that we had much more freedom. My parents were reasonably happy with the situation – Paula's father was a teacher, so *must* be respectable – and let me stay there whenever I wanted. Although my mother did complain that they never saw me. If she knew half of what we got up to, she wouldn't have been happy.

One evening, Paula's mum asked why we didn't bring our conquests back to the house, rather than whatever we were doing. We looked at each other, rather embarrassed. From that moment on, we were unstoppable.

When I stayed, I shared Paula's room. It was very large, so we moved the two beds to opposite ends, and at weekends, hung a makeshift curtain between them. We soon found we could easily ignore the other activity going on in the room. Although some of the guys we brought home found it very disconcerting!

One or other of us occasionally saw the same guy for a few weeks, but that was the exception, rather than the rule. And we always told each other what we'd got up to. We were learning all the way. We began to think we were experts. But then I met Daniel; he showed me I was still a novice.

I'd first seen him in one of the clubs we visited. He seemed to be a regular; often on his own, but known to lots of the clientele, who always nodded or said hello. I hadn't paid much attention at first, but one evening when I hadn't found anyone else, I saw him looking at me. I smiled and held his gaze. He raised his glass and turned back to the bar. We'd joined up with a group from college, and guys were thin on the ground.

"Anyone know who he is?" I asked.

"Who?"

"The guy sitting at the bar with the black trousers and Nehru shirt."

"On the end?"

"Yeah."

There was a general shaking of heads. But one girl, whose name I couldn't remember, laughed.

"I don't know his name, but he's a regular. Has a bit of a reputation. I'd steer clear of him, he's only after one thing."

I looked at Paula, and we had to stop ourselves laughing. What were we all doing in this dive if we weren't after the same thing? Apparently, we hadn't got ourselves the same reputation. We weren't quite sure how. The club gradually filled up, and as our group splintered, I looked over to the guy at the bar a few times. Occasionally, I caught him watching me, but he wasn't embarrassed. Merely smiled. When I went to the bar a while later, I decided to head in his direction. He moved aside to let me in.

"Thanks," I said.

"You're welcome. You don't appear to be having much fun."

"Oh, I'm fine."

"Not seen anyone interesting?"

"Might have."

I smiled as the barman finally appeared, and we fell silent as he slowly got my round. When I'd paid, I went to pick the tray up.

"I'll carry that for you," he offered.

"No thanks, I'm not helpless."

"I can see that. Just being friendly. Come back and have a chat if you get bored."

"I might just do that."

"Promise?"

"No."

When I got back to the table, Paula and one other girl were the only ones left.

"Did you put him in his place?" Paula asked.

"No. We just had a friendly chat."

"That's it?"

"Not necessarily," I replied.

I did spend some time looking around; had a few dances, but no-one appeared who lit my fire. I wandered over to the bar to see if he was still there. He was.

"Hello again," I said.

"Hello. So now you're bored?"

"Not bored, exactly, but it's a bit quiet tonight."

"No-one who does it for you?"

"There might be. I'm not sure yet."

"Ah. I'm Daniel by the way. Dan."

"Hi, Dan, I'm Mary."

"Why don't you sit?" He pulled a bar stool over and put it by him; quite close by him. But I jumped up on it. I was wearing a short skirt, and I knew how to use it. He briefly looked down, and I saw him smile. I looked at him closely for the first time. Quite handsome, in a soft way. Tousled blonde hair, blue eyes. Even though he was sitting down, I could see he was tall and slim, with a confident posture. It was difficult to guess his age, but a few years older than me.

"Thanks. Haven't you found anyone who does it for you, either?" I asked.

"Perhaps I'm not looking."

"Then why come here?"

"True. It's a bit of a dive."

"I'm told you're a regular."

"Are you indeed? Who says so?"

"I have my informants."

"Do you? Do they tell you why I'm here?"

"No. But they think you have a reputation."

"Oh, what for?"

"No idea. They couldn't tell me."

"Is it my reputation that attracted you?"

"Maybe."

He laughed.

"Are you normally so sure of yourself, Mary."

I shrugged.

"Yes, mostly. Do you have a reputation, Dan?"

"Well, it sounds like I must have."

"A reputation for what?"

"Come home and I'll show you. I think you'll enjoy it."

Thinking back now, the world was different then. He could have been a serial killer for all I knew. But then, what is life without taking a few risks. I went over to Paula.

"Don't wait up," I said.

"OK, but give us a call in the morning."

"Yes, will do."

I returned to Dan, and we walked out of the club.

"Is it far?" I asked.

"No, just a short walk."

A couple of corners later, he stopped at a large terraced house, opened the front door, and ushered me into a dark hallway. Climbing the stairs to the first floor, he opened another door, and it closed behind us. I recognised the smell immediately. A mixture of joss sticks and weed.

"Fancy a glass of red?" He asked.

"Yeah."

He showed me into the living room and wandered off. I looked around; not quite hippy style, but close.

"There you go," he said as he handed me a glass. "Want a smoke?"

I'd had a few joints, both at Paula's house and elsewhere. I wasn't really into it. It didn't seem to affect me very much, but what the hell.

"Yeah, I guess."

He opened a box on a side table and took one out. Lighting it, he took a slow draw and handed it to me. I lifted it to my lips and inhaled. It was a different taste than those I'd had previously, and a good deal stronger. I coughed.

"Your first?"

"No. But different."

"Ah, this is good stuff. I have a special source. Don't inhale too hard."

I put the joint back to my lips and inhaled slowly. This time, I managed to draw a small amount into my lungs and felt the effect almost immediately. My head seemed to spin for a few seconds but then return to normal.

"That's better. Now just relax."

"I've heard about men like you."

"I'm not trying to knock you out and ravish you, if that's what you mean."

"Aren't you?"

"No. For what I had in mind, it's far better if you're fully awake. Just a little relaxed."

"What did you have in mind?"

"Oh, nothing much. Just some mind-blowing sex."

I giggled. The weed was having an effect. I felt very relaxed and was feeling horny too. The flat was warm and comfortable. Dan was relaxed and unthreatening. He seemed different to the guys I'd been with up to now. Most had wanted to get right down to action. Dan wasn't pushing at all. In fact, he was lying back on the sofa, eyes closed, taking an occasional drag on the joint before passing it back to me.

"Don't have too much if you're not used to it. A little enhances the desire; too much can wipe it out."

I took a couple of slower puffs and returned it to him. I could feel how relaxed I was. The giggly phase had gone. I now felt deeply calm; slightly spaced out, but very aware of everything around me. Of my own body, now anticipating some pleasure. Of Dan, wondering what he had in mind.

We laid there for what seemed like an age. After a while, I realised I was very horny, but not in an urgent way. Not desperate. Just a deep feeling of need. I started to move towards him. Even though his eyes were still closed, he sensed my approach.

"Is it working, then?"

"Yeah, I need something."

"What's that?"

"You."

He opened his eyes and turned his head towards me.

"Let me lead. I promise it will be worth it."

I agreed. I just wanted to get naked and get on with it, but I was intrigued. What did he have in mind? By now, I'd had sex with more than my fair share of guys; some good, some okay, some instantly forgettable. But most of those encounters had been frantic, at least to begin with. Dan was so laid back, he was almost horizontal.

"Right, why don't you strip off, and I'll get things ready."

This surprised me a bit, but I complied, standing up and removing my clothes. I was no shrinking violet and was soon naked. Meanwhile, Dan unrolled a futon, and put some oil in a bowl; lighting a nightlight underneath it. When he'd done that, he looked at my naked body, smiled, and proceeded to strip himself. I watched intently and was a little disappointed when he removed his briefs to see that his dick was completely soft. My face must have betrayed my thoughts.

"Don't worry," he said. "Watch."

I looked at his dick, not knowing what I was looking for. But slowly, it swelled. The blood flowing into it, engorging its veins.

It grew bigger and bigger. I was watching intently now, wondering how much further it would go. It was the biggest dick I'd come across, and it was still growing.

"Happier now?" He asked.

"Yeah." I couldn't hide my grin.

"Keep watching."

I did, and it started to drop. Slowly, it softened and shrank. Almost back to its original size. I was baffled; I'd never seen anything like it.

"Wow," I said, not having anything else to say.

"I know it's a bit unusual. But it'll be there whenever we need it; there's no hurry. Why don't you lie down, and I'll give you a massage?"

Well, this was different, but I felt relaxed and warm. There was a certain appeal to having a naked man with a big dick massage my naked body. I stretched out on my front on the futon. He straddled me; his soft dick lying on my bum.

"Ready?"

Warm oil dribbled onto my back. My mood meant that I was very conscious of my body; of every sensation. Probably the weed. He set the bowl down, and I finally felt his hands on my back, stroking and caressing. Over my shoulders, down my spine. Up and down my arms and over my neck. I wriggled a bit to get completely comfortable and just gave in to the feelings. He knew what he was doing; soft enough to be teasing at times. Hard enough for it to work into the muscles.

After a while, he shifted position, moving down to straddle my legs. He dribbled more oil over my bum, and I felt it running down between my legs. His hands started on my lower back and worked on over my bum. He massaged my cheeks and thighs; it felt wonderful, but I knew I needed more. He worked his way down my legs, spending time on my calves and feet.

"Spread your legs."

He knelt between them, coming back up to massage my bum again. But now, he let his hands, covered in warm oil, explore further. First, his fingers ran between my cheeks and over my asshole. No guy had touched me there before – I hadn't explored it myself - and I was surprised by how sensitive it was. Then they worked their way down between my legs. First on my thighs, but gradually getting closer and closer to my sex. Finally, his fingers rolled over it and I nearly had an instant orgasm but didn't want it yet.

"Relax," Dan said. "Let it happen. There's plenty of time."

So I did, as he gently concentrated on my sex. Just using the tips of his fingers to massage my lips and clit. I started to feel my orgasm coming, deeper than normal. I came with several strong shudders, my whole body responding to his touch. It was one of the most intense orgasms I'd ever had. Not a short, sharp climax, but a climb to a peak and a slow fall the other side, lasting what seemed like minutes. He moved his hands away and continued to stroke my bum and thighs while I recovered.

"Turn over," he said.

He had a gentle smile on his face; his dick was still flaccid. Once again, he straddled me and poured oil over my torso. Gently stroking my breasts and rubbing my hard nipples. Looking down at me. For once, I felt a little shy and closed my eyes. Giving in to my feelings.

Working down my tummy, he shifted position and moved down to my legs. Finally reaching my feet, he concentrated on them, and I realised how sensitive they were. His fingers worked on my toes and soles. The sensations were a crazy mix. Almost too much, and very intense.

He stopped, and I opened my eyes. He was knelt by my side now; still smiling. Placing one hand on my tummy, he put the other between my legs; I instantly opened them. While he stroked my tummy, occasionally moving up over my breasts, the other hand circled my sex, never quite touching, but always near.

Gradually that hand moved down until he reached my lips. He slid his fingers up and down, spreading them. Two fingers pushing into the opening of my pussy. I spread my legs a little more, and those two fingers entered me, making me gasp. They moved inside me, gently stroking the sensitive lining. Turning his hand, so that he reached different areas. Suddenly, a different sensation grew. His fingers were rubbing the area behind my clit, and I squirmed as he did so.

"Good?" He asked.

"Mmm. Yes." I managed, before falling silent again.

Then he touched my clit, and I was nearly gone. Fingers in me, doing God knows what. Others teasing my clit. I gave in and cried out as my orgasm overtook me. I expected him to stop, but instead, I felt his fingers move more strongly in me, moving in and out quite forcefully. Before I knew it, I reached another orgasm. Different; not as strong. As I came down, he stopped and gently removed his fingers, laying them on my tummy. I just lay there, getting my breath back.

"OK?" He asked after a while.

"Wow. Yeah."

"Good. Fancy a drink?"

He got up and fetched our glasses and the bottle, as well as his little box. He helped me sit up, and we settled on the futon, drinking wine, and smoking another joint. It was all a bit surreal. I was in heaven. Warm, comfortable, and incredibly sexy. I'd had two or three orgasms in a short space of time, and we hadn't even screwed yet. I tried to snuggle up to him, but he didn't really respond so I just leaned against him. We sat there, drinking and smoking in silence.

After a while, I looked down at his dick. I wanted it. Reaching down, I started to stroke his thigh, and he opened his legs a little. As I played with his balls, his dick began to grow, and I stared intently. By the time it was hard, I had begun to wonder how I was going to take it all.

"You're quite big."

"So I gather."

"Do you ever have trouble?"

"How do you mean?"

"Well, is it sometimes … too big?"

"Oh. No. Never had a problem. I'll let you have control. Do you want to?"

"Uh, yeah."

He moved forward and laid on the floor, his dick sticking up. I'd been on top before, but then the action had been more urgent. I'd not had time to think about it. As I moved to straddle him, I couldn't help wondering how I was going to cope with it. I was still very wet, so I didn't worry about that.

Positioning myself over him, I guided the tip between my pussy lips and slowly lowered myself until the head was inside me. It was tight already. Sliding slowly up and down, I went a bit further each time, taking more and more. It was working me up and I was surprised how quickly I got all the way down until I was sitting on his hips. My pussy filled with his thick dick. He smiled up at me.

"See. No problem."

"Yeah. That feels fab."

I started to slide up and down, but he stopped me.

"Rock backwards and forwards. Rub yourself here." He took my hand and moved it to his pubic bone. I got the idea.

I rocked as he'd suggested, and immediately saw why. I immediately began building again. Leaning further forward, I pressed harder against him. With his great dick filling me, and my clit rubbing against him, I didn't last long. A wonderful orgasm engulfed me, and I collapsed onto him. He lay there, letting me come down.

"Don't you need to come?" I asked him eventually.

"Do you want me to?"

The question struck me as odd. Here was a guy who'd picked me up, given me several orgasms, yet didn't seem to need anything in return.

"Well, yeah. I thought it was the usual idea."

He laughed. His dick was still buried in me, and I felt the tremors as he did so.

"I'm not usual."

"No. I'm beginning to see that."

"But I wouldn't want to disappoint you."

He flipped me over onto my back, dick still in me, and lifted my legs over his shoulders. Slowly he started to slide in and out; long slow strokes. His balls hitting my bum on every stroke. I watched him; then watched his dick sliding in and out. My breathing was getting heavier as I realised I was going to come again.

He speeded up and as I reached orgasm, he exploded inside me. His dick seemed to grow even bigger and it twitched and jerked. I felt his cum hit my insides, which gave my orgasm an extra boost. As I came down, he lowered my legs, still smiling.

"Is that better?"

"Well, yeah. But is it better for you?"

I was becoming intrigued by his apparent control.

"Yes. It's good."

When he pulled out, I looked down and was amazed at the mess. I thought I'd wet myself but quickly saw that wasn't it. He reached over for some tissues.

"The bathroom is the first door in the hallway," he said.

"Thanks. Looks like I need it."

I grabbed a couple of tissues, and, holding them in place, went off to clean up. The one advantage of condoms was that most of the mess stayed with the man. They were the ones who had to do the cleaning up. But I preferred it now I was on the pill. No messing about; no awkward pauses and peace of mind.

When I came back, he had another joint ready, and he asked if I was staying the night. As it was about two in the morning, it seemed the best thing to do. We didn't go to bed; just stayed up and talked. He told me that his mother was a yoga teacher and had trained him virtually from birth. He practised it every day. But he'd found in his teen years that he could use it to control virtually every aspect of his body; including his dick. Now he could keep it soft, keep it hard, and come virtually at will. Later, during the night, he showed me.

Dan and I saw each other for a few months. He taught me a lot about my own body and about men's bodies. About how to control our urges and impulses; if we wanted to. But it was this very control that led us to drift apart. I became unnerved by his lack of emotion.

He never grabbed me, bent me over and took me. He never held me passionately; indeed, we never really kissed. He gave me the best orgasms I'd had so far, and we'd both agreed we weren't looking for anything serious. But this lack of connection eventually struck me as odd; cold.

He'd been a great teacher, but I needed something more.

Chapter 3 – A Wedding and a Funeral

Catherine had fallen head over heels in love. Tony was considerably older than her and seemed a bit of an old-fashioned charmer. He was just the sort of man that I imagined her ending up with. She had – to me – a childish view of love and marriage. I guess to her, I was promiscuous. We were very different in that way.

But she met Tony, and that was it. She was smitten. I liked him too; at least, he seemed perfect for Catherine. He was handsome, in a rather dated way; more fifties heartthrob than seventies romantic. Tall, well-built, and always smartly dressed. I don't think I ever saw him in jeans or a t-shirt.

He treated our parents well, and they liked him from the first meeting. Within six months, they were engaged, and plans for the wedding were started. Mum and Dad were not well off, so Tony paid for most of it himself. This caused a bit of embarrassment to Dad, but Tony gently persuaded him that it was not unusual, and dad relented.

He was a bit of a mystery from the beginning. Catherine didn't ask questions, but he was always vague about his family. He didn't seem to have any. What he did was always vague too. He talked about 'business', but it was never specified. He never seemed short of money, though, and Catherine and our parents were impressed by that, so I didn't interfere.

I was asked to be a bridesmaid, which I accepted. It did mean, however, that Catherine and I had to spend more time together than usual, and I found it hard. I had to keep reminding myself that it was Catherine's wedding, so I had to fit in with her decisions.

We spent several weekends traipsing around the wedding shops looking at wedding dresses and then searching for dresses for the bridesmaids. There were three of us. Me, and two girls from the bank where Catherine worked; Jane and Anne. I got the impression that they shared her views on my life, but it didn't bother me too much.

The dress she eventually selected was beautiful. But the bridesmaid's dresses ... A shade of shocking pink that I thought only existed in the world of Barbie, and even her two friends weren't that keen. But it was her day, so we went for the fittings, and tried not to look in the mirror too often. Mum found an outfit that she loved, but it was expensive, so this time, I bought it for her.

***

Three months before the wedding, I got a call from Mum saying that Dad wasn't well. I went home to find that he'd not been feeling well for a while but hadn't done anything about it.

When he finally went to the doctor, he was immediately referred for tests. Lung cancer. He was going in for an operation the following week.

He seemed fine in himself, but I could see he was worried, and Mum was too. For the only time I could remember, Catherine was being a bit selfish. For all her faults, she was a compassionate and caring girl. But I guess she thought her big day was approaching and Dad might ruin it. So, she wasn't being very supportive.

One evening, I took her aside.

"Kate, how is Dad, really?"

"Oh, he's OK. After the op, he'll be fine."

"That's a bit optimistic, isn't it?"

"Well, that's what he's saying."

"And you believe him?"

She looked at me, clearly annoyed.

"Why shouldn't I?"

"He's got lung cancer, and he left it a long time before getting it looked at. It's serious, Kate."

"No, he'll be fine."

That was the end of the conversation. I still don't know whether she really believed what he'd told her, or if she had tried to blank it all out.

He had the operation, and I went in to see him in the evening after I finished work. Mum was sat by the bed, Dad was asleep, but I instantly knew from her face that things weren't good.

"Hi, Mum." I gave her a hug. "How is he?"

She gave me a strained look.

"They've taken out a lung. But it's spread."

"Oh ..."

We sat silently for a few minutes, both lost in our thoughts.

"What happens now?" I asked.

"I'm not sure. I think they'll tell us over the next few days."

They did and it wasn't good. We all sat by his bed, while a doctor explained the options. The cancer had spread and was aggressive. It would kill him in a few months. He told Dad about chemo and radiotherapy. But they would only buy him time, not get rid of it; it was too late for that. In the end, he left it to us to discuss, and for Dad to decide what he wanted to do. I already knew what he would do. The reality of the situation had now struck Kate. After the four of us had talked it around for a while, I decided Mum and Dad should be left alone to discuss it.

"Mum, Kate and I will go and wait in reception. Take as long as you want."

I almost dragged Kate away.

"Why did you do that?"

"Because the decision should be theirs, not ours."

We walked along the endless hospital corridors. In reception, we grabbed a coffee and sat down.

"I guess you were right," Kate said.

"Unfortunately."

"What do you think he'll do?"

"Nothing."

"What, no treatment?" She seemed shocked.

"No. He'll just accept fate."

"But why would he refuse it? He'll live longer."

"You heard about the side effects; they're horrible. And for what? A few extra months?"

We sat quietly for what seemed hours, and Mum finally appeared, looking around for us. When she came over, I could see she had been crying.

"Want to sit down, or go home, Mum?"

"Home."

"OK."

We walked to the car slowly.

"He doesn't want treatment," Mum finally said.

"Did you expect him to?"

She paused.

"No, not really. I understand why."

And that was it. He left hospital a week or so later. He was his old self. He never lost his positive outlook, and anyone who offered him sympathy got short shrift. He was determined to make the most of what time he had left and that centred on Catherine's wedding.

***

A few weeks before the event, we had a practice in the church. Everyone was there; Tony and Catherine, we three bridesmaids, Mum and Dad. And Tony's best man; Mike. I noticed Mike immediately. Most girls would. He was almost the opposite of Tony. Very trendy, younger, big hair. Just my type. The other two bridesmaids were quite interested as well. After the rehearsal, we went to the pub next to the church for a drink and a quiet chat. At one point, Mike came over to where I was sitting.

"Hi, Mary."

"Hello, Mike. That seemed to go well."

"Yes. It's all quite easy really."

"Have you known Tony long?"

"Oh, a while."

"Do you work with him?"

"Sometimes."

He was proving as vague as Tony, so I stopped pushing.

"You're not much like your sister."

"No, we're very different in a lot of ways."

"Single, I gather."

"Been asking, have you?"

"Well, best men have a reputation to keep up when it comes to bridesmaids."

I smiled.

"What about Jane and Anne?"

"Think I should try?"

"Depends what you want."

"How so?"

"If you're happy to spend time buying them drinks while they flutter their eyelashes and giggle, you might get a peck on the cheek at the end of the evening."

"And you're different?"

"Who knows?"

"That sounds like a challenge."

"Does it?"

He was smiling now.

"Yes, and you know exactly what you're doing."

"Always, Mike. Always."

***

By the day of the wedding, Dad had deteriorated. He was thin and rather breathless but determined to enjoy his eldest daughter's big day. Catherine had been completely wrapped up in the wedding, and I'm not sure she had noticed Dad's frailty. She, Jane and Anne had spent an eternity fussing over every last detail, and I was largely excluded. I was happy to leave them to it. Determined to play my part on the day, but also try and support Mum and Dad as well.

The day started early. Jane and Anne appeared at seven in the morning. God knows why; the wedding wasn't until two in the afternoon. They went into Catherine's room, and the three of them were closeted there for hours. The hairdresser came, and did our hair; quite well, I must admit.

I put on my underwear in my own room. I'd chosen a nice white lace set which fitted rather well. If I had to look like a giant lump of candy floss, at least I could feel good underneath. When I finished putting on my make-up, I slipped on a dressing gown to go to Catherine's room.

They were all in their underwear as well, not wanting to risk staining the dresses while they got ready. Catherine had a white bridal set on, clearly not used to such fripperies. The bra wasn't a perfect fit, and her stockings were pulled up too high, but she did look like the virgin bride she almost certainly was.

I was a bit surprised to see that Jane and Anne had very ordinary nude tights on, and what must have been their everyday bras and knickers. I took my gown off, to put my dress on.

"You're wearing stockings," Jane said.

"Uh, yes."

"Only the bride wears stockings."

"Why? Who's going to know?"

"Why did you buy stockings?"

"I always wear them. I hate tights."

"What?" Anne asked. "Every day?" The bewilderment was clear in her voice.

"Yes."

They both looked at me as if I was an alien; or, more probably in their eyes, a slut. I could live with that. Later on, I noticed that Anne, who was very dark, still had visible hairs on her legs. Visible even through her tights, which weren't exactly sheer.

I also noticed that Catherine was excited but very nervous. Once or twice, I looked at her and she seemed very thoughtful. It was one of the few times when I wished we had been closer, and I could have worked out what she was thinking. But Jane and Anne were jabbering all the time, and I couldn't stick it for long.

When the time came, Catherine looked lovely. We three bridesmaids? Not so much. The colour of our dresses suited none of us, and we looked like something out of a three-year-old's drawing of a princess. But it wasn't our day; it was Catherine's.

The day went largely as expected. Catherine was a few minutes late, both she and Tony fluffed one line in their vows, and the photographer was a tyrant who bossed everyone around for half an hour after the ceremony. At the church, and later at the reception, I noticed that almost all the guests were from our family. There were just a handful from Tony's side, and most turned out to be friends of his. I didn't find anyone who was related to him; he was still a bit of a mystery. And Mike was there, of course.

The first time I saw him, I was following Catherine up the aisle. He was standing by Tony and looked back as we approached them. He saw me and winked; I smiled. I still had hope that this day might not be as boring as I feared. He and Tony were very smartly turned out, and it was the first time I had seen the groom in truly fashionable clothes. Albeit the formal wear of a wedding. Mike looked as if he had come straight out of a new romantics' video.

The reception was typical of the time; a sit-down, four-course meal at a local hotel. All very formal and stiff. As Tony's parents weren't around, all three bridesmaids were at the top table, but when I got there, I found that Mike had been seated at the opposite end to me with Jane. I was stuck right on the other end, next to Anne. I don't think we did more than exchange forced pleasantries for two hours. Perhaps I should have been a little more involved in the planning.

I had been watching Dad carefully, but he was holding up well. I saw him look over at Catherine a few times, with a look of proud satisfaction. I knew he was nervous about his speech, but he had written it alone, not allowing anyone to help, or, as far as I knew, see it beforehand.

When he finally got up to speak, he was shaking slightly, but he gave a short, beautiful, thoughtful speech, which brought a tear or two to my eyes. I'm sure Catherine and Mum were similarly affected. Tony's speech was very assured and full of his usual bonhomie.

Finally, Mike got to his feet and lightened the mood, as was his traditional duty. He read the telegrams (yes, we still had them in those days), and then went into a bit of a shaggy dog story about how he had met Tony, and what a great guy he was. How much of it was true, I still don't know. But it was entertaining, and he soon had the guests laughing.

He paid tribute to Catherine, bringing out the usual guff about her being the perfect match for Tony. At the end, he thanked the bridesmaids, who had made the whole day run smoothly and assisted Catherine on her big day.

I breathed a sigh of relief as the formal part came to an end. There was now a little time before the disco began, and I wanted to take a break. I checked on Mum and Dad; they were going to have a lie down for an hour. I went up to my room, took the dress off, kicked off my shoes, and did the same. After a few minutes, there was a knock on the door. I threw on my dressing gown and opened the door to find Mike standing in the corridor.

"Hi, Mary."

"Hello, Mike."

"You disappeared quickly, I just wanted to make sure you were okay."

"Really?"

"Yes. Is that wrong?"

"I'm fine. Just wanted an hour without my shoes and that damned dress."

"Lovely colour. Did you choose it?"

"What do you think?"

"I'm guessing the maiden aunts did."

I thought for a second, then smiled. "Maiden aunts?"

"If they're not now, they will be in a few years."

"That's a bit harsh."

"True though, and you know it."

"Did you want anything, Mike?"

"Not right now, thank you ..."

I realised I could have phrased the question better.

"... later perhaps."

I had to admire his cheek.

"Oh, and you look much better out of that dress."

I'm not sure what possessed me, but I let go of the door, undid my robe, and pushed it off my shoulders, allowing it to drop to the floor. For the first time, I saw from his expression that I had caught him by surprise. I followed his eyes as he looked me up and down in my underwear. I was silently pleased with my choice.

"Oh, I know I do, Mike. See you later."

I gently closed the door, even though I would have loved to see what his response would have been. I stood still, and a few seconds later, I heard him walk away. Feeling much brighter, I laid back on the bed and thought about the game Mike and I had implicitly agreed to play this evening. We hadn't agreed on any rules, but I was pretty sure it would probably be a welcome draw.

I reached the ballroom as the evening guests began to arrive; there weren't a huge number who hadn't been invited to the wedding. It turned out to be mainly more of Catherine's bank colleagues.

"Where have you been?" I turned and saw Anne standing in front of me.

"Sorry?"

"You're supposed to be helping your sister."

"Does she need any help?"

For the first time, she looked a little unsure of herself.

"I'm not sure."

"What do you mean?"

"She and Tony went upstairs for ten minutes to freshen up, and when they came down, she looked upset. I don't know what happened."

I could guess. Anne bugged me. I lost my tact.

"I guess Tony wanted a quickie, and Catherine didn't."

She opened her mouth, closed it again. Opened it again.

"A ... quickie?" She was grasping at the concept, which seemed a mystery to her. I finally saw realisation on her face. "He wouldn't. He's a good man."

I sighed. She'd just confirmed everything I had guessed about her.

"God, we all need a quickie sometimes, don't we, Anne?"

And I left her there; I really didn't want to hear her answer. But I did feel I needed to see Catherine. I went over to where she and her new husband were standing to greet the last new guests.

"Hello, Mrs Crowther," I said lightly, coming up behind her. She turned, and I was a bit taken aback by her face. She had clearly been crying. "Are you all right?"

"Yes, Mary, I'm fine." She was very tight.

"No, you're not. What's wrong?"

"Nothing."

"Catherine, we may not be close…" I held up my hand as she went to respond, "…but I know when something's wrong."

I tapped Tony's shoulder, and he turned his head. "I'm taking Catherine upstairs to tidy up her make-up. Won't be long." He nodded and turned away again. She protested a bit but followed me when I grabbed her hand.

The next fifteen minutes were the nearest thing we ever had to a real heart-to-heart. Looking back, it almost breaks my heart. My guess had been right, and she had been mortified. I soon realised that she knew next to nothing about sex. Even seemed ignorant about the mechanics.

I tried, in ten minutes flat, to explain as much as I could to her. Then tried to explain how wonderful it could be; the best thing in the world. How they should work at it together so they could both enjoy it. But the idea that she could enjoy it seemed to baffle her. And we didn't have time for me to go into such a delicate area.

I tidied her make-up and we moved towards the door. She stopped, and I turned around.

"Mary?"

"Yes."

"I know I've not really been a great big sister to you. But we're just so different. I know you think I disapprove of what you get up to, and perhaps I do. I must seem very naïve to you. But right now, I wish I had some of your experience."

I smiled.

"You're right. We've chosen different lives. I have quite a lot of experience, as you put it, and I don't regret any of it. I can only guess how you're feeling about tonight. But with Tony, you've found a guy who seems to worship you. Go with it; do everything you can to enjoy it. Sex is a partnership."

She came up to me. "Thank you, Mary. I'm sure it will all be okay."

As we went back down, I thought about those last words. I wasn't very confident she was right.

In the ballroom, the DJ was playing some background music, and Tony was at the door waiting for Catherine.

"All ready? I was wondering what you two were up to."

"Just a sisterly chat," she replied and took his hand. I smiled, and hung back, as the newlyweds made their entrance. Mike was standing with the DJ and took the microphone to announce the arrival of Mr & Mrs Crowther. The guests dutifully clapped, and Tony led Catherine to the centre of the dancefloor.

They had chosen 'Fly me to the moon' by Frank Sinatra; it wouldn't have been my choice, but it wasn't my wedding. They danced it well enough, and then others started to take the floor. The track set the mood for much of the night, though. A lot of older music; mostly good but lost on a lot of the guests.

I saw Mum and Dad dancing and stopped to watch them. A few relatives who we only saw at weddings and funerals had already approached me, asking if Dad was okay. They'd noticed the change in him. I'd lightly replied that he'd not been well; he hadn't wanted people to know he was dying.

Jane and Anne were sitting at a table near the bar; conspicuously alone. Very conspicuous, as we three still had our awful pink dresses on. You couldn't miss us in a blackout.

"Can I get you a drink?"

I turned, smiling. "Hello, Mike. I'm all right, thanks."

"From what I saw earlier, I'd have to agree."

The game had started.

"So, do I get to see more of you?"

"You might, but you've got to pass a test or two first."

"Test?"

"Mmm. Up for it?"

"What's the prize?"

"You might get to unwrap what you saw earlier."

He chuckled. "Are we playing games, then?"

"Perhaps. Depends if you want it enough."

"I think I do. What's the test?"

"Oh, there'll be a few. Want the first?"

"Ready."

I turned around to look at my fellow bridesmaids.

"The maiden aunts."

He frowned. "What about them?"

"Before the evening's out, I want to see you dance with each of them twice. And close dances, too. And try to look as if you're enjoying it."

"Seriously?"

"Well, you are the best man. You're supposed to look after the bridesmaids, aren't you?"

"Can't I just look after one?"

"Those two first."

He grinned. "I hope you're worth it."

"You'd better be, too."

I went off to do my duty by speaking to some distant relatives. I saw Mike grab one of Tony's friends, and they went over to Jane and Anne. The girls simpered, as the guys led them to the dance floor. Well, he was trying.

I circulated for an hour or so. At that point, Mum came over and said that she and Dad were leaving for their room. Dad was sitting at a table, exhausted. I found Catherine and Tony, and they went to say goodnight to my parents, who then slipped quietly out of the room.

By now, quite a lot of drink had been consumed in some quarters. I found myself sitting with a couple of girls I didn't know. I discovered they worked at the bank with Catherine.

"That's a very … bright pink, isn't it?" One of them asked, slurring slightly.

"Yes, not my choice, really."

"How do you know Catherine?"

"I'm her sister."

"Oh, you must be Mary. I'm Sarah, this is Linda." The other girl murmured a greeting. "Mind you, it suits you better than the two virgins."

I turned sharply towards her. "Who?"

"Oh, sorry, Jane and Anne. Perhaps I shouldn't have said that."

"No, it's fine." After a few seconds, a thought struck me. "Am I right in guessing that before today they were the three virgins?"

Sarah looked embarrassed. "Oops, sorry. I wasn't thinking. I didn't mean to offend you."

"Oh, don't worry, you haven't. Perhaps if my sister has found someone, those two will as well."

Linda leaned across Sarah. "Have you spent any time with them?"

"A bit."

"And?"

"They do seem rather … naïve."

"Naïve? Ha. I doubt they take their knickers off to have a shower. They wouldn't know a dick if it was waved in their faces."

Sarah sniggered. "And they certainly wouldn't know what to do with it. Even with an instruction manual."

Linda swayed in again. "An instruction manual with pictures."

They both giggled again. Finally, Sarah straightened up. "I pity any man who tries it on with them. Waste of time."

I thought about the first task I had set Mike and smiled. Time to find out how he was getting on.

I finally spotted him chatting to a small group by the bar. He saw me, and made his excuses, before heading in my direction.

"Hello, Mike. How are you getting on?"

"You might well ask. Can I get you a drink?"

"Actually, yes. A glass of any wine you can find, please."

"Take a seat; I'll see what I can do."

I sat down at the nearest empty table, again glad to take the weight off my feet. Or more particularly, these new shoes, which I should have worn in more. I looked around. Small groups here and there; a few people still dancing, but rather wearily.

"There you go; that was all I could find."

"Thanks. Seems to be going okay."

"Yes. Just like every other wedding you've ever been to."

"Mmm. So, have you been keeping Jane and Anne company?"

"God, they're awful."

"Are they?"

"Yes, and you knew it."

"Well, I felt a bit sorry for them sitting all on their own."

"It's not surprising though, is it? They've got to be two of the most boring women I've met in a long time. How does Catherine know them?"

I told him, and then related my chat with Sarah and Linda.

"Is Catherine as ... err, the same as them?"

I thought for a moment.

"I have to admit, she might be. She's very ... naïve."

We both went quiet for a while, probably dealing with roughly the same thoughts. Finally, I leaned nearer to him.

"Mike, you've known Tony for a long time, yes?"

"Mmm."

"And from what I've seen of him, he's no innocent. He's a bit old-fashioned, at least for me, but I'm guessing he's got a bit of a history. We don't know anything about him. But what the hell does he see in Catherine? She was smitten from the start. Too bloody innocent to see the dangers. She needs a guy who's as boring and naïve as she is. She's terrified about tonight; no idea what to expect." He looked at me quizzically. "No idea at all, believe me."

"So, they haven't ...?"

"Nope. I doubt they've done anything at all. Now, you're not going to tell me Tony's a virgin as well?"

Mike suppressed a smile. "Uh, no. No, I don't believe he is."

"I bet he's not. Nor am I. I've been around; you worked that out. That's why you're interested." He grinned. "And I see in him a man who's been around. So why pick Catherine?"

He sat still for a while, thinking. Finally, he looked at me with a serious expression.

"Mary, I hear what you're saying, but I'm not going to tell you about Tony if he's chosen not to. All I will say is that, yes, he has had something of a difficult life. And probably done a few things that didn't look good in hindsight. What I will say is that you can trust him to look after Catherine. He may not be the best husband in the world, particularly if she is as naïve as you say, but he will see she's provided for and cared for."

I sighed. "That's it? That's all a girl can expect?"

"Mary, it depends on the girl, doesn't it? If Tony had come after you, what would you have done?"

"Turned him away."

"Exactly, but Catherine didn't. He was what she wanted. Should we blame either of them for their choice?"

41

"No. No, I suppose not. I truly hope they're happy."

"And why shouldn't they be? After tonight, you may find that Catherine starts going to wife-swapping parties and the occasional orgy."

The idea made me laugh. "I doubt that, but it's an interesting idea."

We sank into silence, thinking. Mike finally stirred.

"Well, that was all a bit of a downer."

"Yes, sorry."

"Oh, that's okay. You're family; you're bound to want to look out for her. But let's stop talking about what Catherine's going to be doing in bed and think about what her much more experienced sister will be doing."

"*Much* more experienced?"

He grinned. "Aren't you?"

I shrugged. "Yep. Probably am."

"Well, fancy a dance? And you can tell me about all those experiences."

With that, I decided to put my concerns to one side, and enjoy the rest of the evening. I had a good-looking guy on a string here. He wanted me, and I wanted him. I was just going to make him wait.

The DJ was playing more slow records now, as the evening progressed. I had a slow dance with Mike.

"Want me to tell you a story?" I whispered as he held me close.

"What sort of story?"

As we danced, I made up a little erotic tale, whispering it to him. Explicit, rough, as wild as I could come up with. When the song ended, I separated from him.

"You must introduce me to your friends, Mike."

He looked a bit bewildered as I led him to where his group were seated. He recovered enough to introduce the four guys sitting around a table. We made a few brief pleasantries before I decided on my plan. "So," I said, "who's going to ask me to dance?"

Over the next half an hour, I danced alternately with Mike and each of his friends in turn. Saying little or making small talk with them. But dripping sex into his ear each time I danced with Mike. His reaction was a joy to behold. I think he had been shocked the first time; amused the second. But after that, he was clearly getting more and more worked up; and frustrated. As he held me close, I occasionally felt his erection pressing into me, and the occasional deep breath.

At one point while I was taking a rest, the music died. Mike announced that the bride and groom were leaving the party. I went over and kissed Catherine and Tony. I could see the fear in her eyes. Moments later, they were gone.

"Well, they're off to have fun."

I turned to look at him sternly.

"Sorry, my little joke. Now. Have we stopped storytelling? Can we get onto the real thing?"

I was ready but still wanted to make him wait.

"You're the best man, Mike. You can't leave quite yet. How about two of your friends offer the maiden aunts a slow dance?"

He gave me a look of amazement. "How am I going to persuade them to do that?"

"Up to you, Mike."

He looked hard at me; a faint smile on his lips. "I really hope it's worth it."

"So do I, Mike."

He wandered over to his mates, and shortly afterwards, two of them went over to Jane and Anne, who were happily escorted to the dancefloor. There weren't many people left, as guests had started to depart. Mike came back.

"Well done."

He shrugged. "They drew lots."

"Ha."

"So?"

"Let's have another dance."

Reluctantly, he led me back to the floor, and we danced close. I looked at Jane and Anne and their respective partners. The girls were trying to do a slow dance without touching their partners. I told Mike; he turned us around so he could see. Then I started whispering in his ear. This time, not a made-up story. This time I gave him instructions. He pulled his head away.

"Seriously?"

"Yup."

And then I told him what we were going to do if he carried them out.

"Ready now?" He asked.

"Give me time to say goodnight to a few people, then give me ten minutes."

I went back to my room, took my dress off, shoved it into the wardrobe and freshened up. I checked myself in the full-length mirror. I must admit, I liked what I saw. I smiled as I waited for Mike. I wanted him, but it was a deep need; I wasn't desperate. I was still going to have some fun teasing him when he arrived.

There was an urgent rap on the door. I walked towards it slowly; I knew that if he had followed instructions, he wanted it to open as soon as possible,

I looked through the spyhole. He'd followed instructions. He was standing there holding an ice bucket with a bottle and two glasses in it. Completely naked. Nervously moving his head from side to side checking the corridor was still empty. I spent a few seconds checking him out, but the spyhole distorted the image.

"Who is it?"

"For Christ's sake, Mary, it's me."

I slowly opened the door, and even in his worried state, he took the time to look me up and down quickly. I slowly did the same to him. I liked what I saw. Fit, well-built, and his dick … Well, I'd felt it against me a few times earlier in the evening, but even in its half-mast state, it looked huge.

"Hello, Mike."

"Can I come in?" He was still taking in my body, but also checking the corridor.

I nodded towards the ice bucket. "Champagne?"

"Yes."

"Come in, then."

He gave a sharp kick, and a pile of clothes flew from the floor of the corridor into the room. He followed rapidly, and I shut the door. He visibly relaxed.

"Christ, Mary. I was shitting myself. Where shall I put this?"

"Hold on to it for a while."

"What?"

He stood in the open space between the door and the bed, holding the ice bucket. I walked slowly around him, admiring his physique. No spare weight, toned with a nice, tight bum. I stood behind him and let my hand stray across his buttocks; he flinched.

"You look good, Mike."

"I know."

I moved around to his front and looked down at his dick.

"You look *very* good."

I moved a few feet away.

"I like what I see. Like what you see?"

He slowly looked me up and down, and grinned.

"Even more than I did this afternoon."

I moved towards him again and stared into his eyes.

"Looks like you're a big boy, too."

"I've never had any complaints."

"Well, let's hope I'm not the first."

I gave him a kiss and slowly dropped to my knees. And came face to face with the biggest dick I'd ever seen. It wasn't yet fully erect, but it was still huge. I gently ran a couple of fingers across his abdomen, and his dick twitched. Dropping them lower, I slowly cupped his balls and lifted them. His dick rose above them, and I moved forward and placed my lips around the head. He flinched. When I looked up, all I could really see was the ice bucket he was still holding.

I pushed my head forward, and my lips slid down his dick, taking more and more in my mouth. I knew that when he was fully erect, there was no way I'd get the whole thing in. I wondered how I'd manage to take it all anywhere else, but I sure wanted to try. He groaned as my lips pulled his foreskin fully back inside my mouth, and I gripped his balls tighter. He opened his legs slightly, to allow me better access, no doubt. It was swelling as I worked on it, hard now.

I moved my hands to his bum and started to move my mouth backwards and forwards along its entire length. Each time I pushed down as far as I could, he gave a little grunt. I couldn't now take the whole length, feeling the tip touching the back of my throat before I reached the bottom. I knew if I tried to take more, I'd gag. Might work for some people, but not me.

I lost myself on the heat in my mouth and moved one hand from his bum down between my legs. I was wet; I knew that. I gently stroked myself. Moving my fingers up and down in time with his dick sliding in and out of my mouth. I could have quite easily come but wasn't in a hurry. Coming off his dick, I licked the end and playfully gave it a gentle bite. He let out a cry. I slowly stood up, one hand still on his dick.

"Sorry. Slipped."

His breathing was a little heavy.

"Yeah, right. Can I put this down?"

"Mmm. Why not? Perhaps open it and fill a couple of glasses?"

I turned around, and walked away from him, deliberately rolling my hips as I did so. I sat on the bed, as he put the bucket on the side table, and set about opening the bottle.

"I'm glad I accepted the challenge, Mary."

"So am I Mike. But just think, you could be in Jane or Anne's room."

He gave an exaggerated shiver. "Careful Mary. Thoughts of them naked is likely to deflate me very quickly."

"I'd find a way to fix it."

He looked down at his dick, not showing any sign of deflating.

"Are you sure you want a glass right now?" He asked, a smile on his face.

"Offering an alternative?"

"I can think of one or two."

I thought quickly. I could carry on teasing him; he was playing along, after all. But I knew he wanted me, and I really wanted to try that dick. I stood up, and slowly removed my bra. I walked up to him and moved close, again wrapping my hand around his dick.

"So how many times will this fire tonight?"

"Enough to fuck you raw."

"We'll see, Mike. Get on the bed; I want to be in charge the first time I ride that monster."

He grinned. "Fine by me; but I need to get condoms out of my jacket."

I must have frowned.

"No offence to you, Mary. But I'm no saint; I'm quite ... active and I don't trust every girl I meet. I don't want to suddenly find I've got five kids, all with different mothers."

I smiled, slipping my knickers off, and he came back with a pack of Durex. Laying down on the bed, he slipped the condom over his dick.

"All yours."

I looked down at it, standing to attention, and looking even bigger now he was lying down. For the first time, I noticed not only its length but its thickness, too. I straddled him and wriggled so that I could place the head against my pussy lips. I rubbed it up and down my opening, and slowly lowered myself onto it. I was glad I was wet.

I moved up and down gingerly, going a little lower each time. I let out the odd gasp as it inched further and further into me, constantly adjusting my position. He had his hands behind his head, watching me, as I impaled myself on his dick. About half-way down, I stopped and leaned forward to kiss him. He put his arms around me.

"Got you now."

"Or have I got you?"

"Who cares?"

I started sliding up and down. Again, going further down with each stroke. It was stretching me; not hurting but giving me sensations I hadn't had before. Suddenly, my clit touched his skin; I was down. I had that whole dick inside me. I relaxed onto him.

"Got to admit, Mike. That feels damn good."

"Mmm. Does, doesn't it?"

I sat back up, forgetting that that would force his dick deeper, and I gasped as the head hit my cervix. Recovering quickly, I knew I just wanted to fuck it. Placing my hands on his abdomen,

I began to rock backwards and forwards, rubbing my clit on his pelvic bone. This was my normal method; it worked well. But not so well with this monster inside me.

With every forward movement, his dick hit my cervix, and if that carried on, it would get painful. And we had a lot more to do before the night was over. So, I leaned down over him, hands either side of his head, and started to slide up and down. It wasn't likely to make me come, but it felt amazing. He moved his hands down to my bum and started squeezing it.

Suddenly, he grabbed my hips and stopped me about halfway on his cock.

"Stay right there."

Then he started to fuck me. He lifted his hips on and off the bed, driving his dick in and out of my pussy. He pulled my bum cheeks apart, which stretched my pussy as well. I gave in, letting him take control. After a while, I realised I was building to orgasm. I rarely came from being fucked alone, but here it was fast approaching. I began to breathe heavily, and he saw it. He speeded up, taking longer strokes.

Suddenly, the heat from my pussy spread, and I bucked as my orgasm took over. My body spasmed several times, and he slowed right down, and let me drop down onto him. He stopped as I came down, stroking my bum. When my breathing evened out, I lifted my head off his chest. "Your turn now."

I sat up and started to ride his dick hard. Sometimes just the head; sometimes all the way down and wriggled my hips with him filling me to the core. He started to groan now, so I bent forward again and rested my hands on the bed. Watching him closely, I moved my hips up and down as hard as I could. He gave a sharp cry, and I felt his dick jerk and spasm inside me.

His whole body jumped, and he let out a long, low groan. I let myself drop down on him, and when I reached the bottom, his dick jerked several more times. We lay for a little while, recovering. I slowly lifted myself off him and flopped down on the bed next to him. He leaned over and gave me a kiss.

"Has that taken the edge off?" He asked.

"For the moment." In truth, I was going to need a rest before tackling that again.

He grabbed the condom on his shrinking dick. "I'll just clean up." He headed to the bathroom.

I grabbed the glasses of champagne and handed him one as he came back.

"Do you mind if I have a joint before round two?" I asked.

"As long as I can share it."

I opened the window, and we sprawled out on the bed, drinking champagne and smoking dope. We said little. There was no hurry; we had all night.

After chilling out, I turned on my side towards him and looked at his dick. He was one of those men whose dick didn't shrink that much when it was flaccid. I reached over and traced my nails up and down its length.

"Does this make all the girls happy?"

"Most of them."

"I'll bet."

"One or two have run scared, though."

"Really?"

"Yea. Bailed out when they saw it."

"Well, I was a bit nervous."

"But you like a challenge. Right?"

"Mmm."

I was gently rubbing my fingers along it now, and it was responding. I lifted it and moved my attention to his balls. They were huge too. Stroking them slowly; gently squeezing them until he let out a little grunt. He went to run his hand up my thigh towards my sex, but I pushed it away.

"You just relax. I want to play with my new toy."

He chuckled. "Be my guest."

I shifted down the bed so that my head was over his groin. Lifting one ball, I put my lips around it, and sucked it in, gently closing my teeth around it. He jumped. I released it.

"You just be a good boy. I wouldn't want to accidentally bite too hard."

"I'll be good." He looked down and smiled.

I took the other ball and enclosed that one with my mouth. I contemplated taking them both, but I knew they were too big to get in my mouth at the same time. So, I continued to suck on one, and use my fingers on the other. His scrotum had tightened, and I licked it from side to side. I turned to his dick and began to work my way up it, using my tongue, my lips, and occasionally nibbling with my teeth.

It was hard again now, and I gently pulled the skin down, exposing the head. Purple and red; smooth and silky. Just below it, the veins ribbed and prominent. I licked the head, running my tongue over the top, around the edge, and poking it into the slit. He was beginning to enjoy my work.

I placed my lips over the whole head and dropped down. I knew I wasn't going to be able to take it all, but I was enjoying it and took as much as I could. Moving up and down; sometimes fast and regular, then slow and subtle. Still playing with his balls with my fingers. Changing the angle, and running my lips up and down one side, then the other. Always returning to licking and sucking the head.

Playing with him was turning me on. I took my hand off his balls. Continuing to work on his cock with my mouth, I reached down and started to play with myself.

"I can help you with that." He was watching what I was doing. He jumped, as I closed my teeth on the edge of his dick. He got the message and dropped his head back down on the bed. I was in control here; lying with my head on his hip, my mouth filled with his dick, bringing myself to orgasm. As I came, my moans were muffled, and he grunted a couple of times; my mouth must have jerked a bit. My body relaxed, and I decided it was time to milk him.

I shifted position so that I had more room to manoeuvre and started to work hard on his cock. Still sliding my lips up and down, but now also using one hand on the part I couldn't take, and the other massaging his balls. I wanted to make him come, but I wasn't sure how much control he had.

I needn't have worried. His balls suddenly tightened more and knew he was close. I shifted slightly and moved my mouth so that my lips were running up and down the side of the head. His body tensed, he groaned. His dick went into spasm and sent a stream of spunk high into the air. And another. And another.

Some come down on my face; some on my back, some on my arms. And still, it came. I was determined not to pull away. Now it was running down my hands, and still coming. I'd never seen so much cum.

Eventually, it ceased, and his body sank back to the bed. He raised his head, and I looked up at him.

"Where did all that come from?"

He laughed. "Sorry. Big balls, lots of cream."

"I think I'd better go and clean up." I got off the bed and went into the bathroom. I burst out in a fit of giggles when I looked in the mirror. It was all over my face, in my hair, on my breasts, my arms, and I knew there was some on my back. My hands were dripping. He appeared in the doorway.

"I must admit, that was a very productive one. Must have been marking my territory."

He grinned as he came over, and we both cleaned up as best as we could.

"Well, if you were, it's only your territory for tonight."

"I'm fine with that; still leaves plenty of time."

We were both quite tired by that time, and mellow from the joint. We curled up in bed and fell asleep. At some point, I woke up blearily, only to feel a hand between my legs, and realised I was already building to orgasm. But he wasn't going to just let me come.

"Awake?" He whispered.

"Yes," I gasped.

"Can I take you?"

"Yes."

Before I knew what was happening, he threw the covers off and physically twisted my body up until I was on my hands and knees. Still half asleep, but feeling incredibly horny, he pushed into me from behind. I pushed my bum back to meet him. I groaned as he filled my pussy and began to fuck me. Full, strong strokes, until I was grunting at every thrust.

I had to slow him a couple of times, as I could fully feel his size at that angle. But eventually, I knew I was going to come and gave up caring. He knew too, grabbed my hips, and started to fuck me hard. As I came, my body bucked, and I cried out. He kept going, through my orgasm, and just as I was coming down, he grunted, and I felt him jerk inside me. I was now used to how many times he spasmed, and he held me up until he had finished. Then, we both sank down to the bed; Mike sliding out as we did so.

I don't remember what happened then. I think I fell straight back to sleep. A wonderful deep sleep.

In the morning we were at it again. But longer and slower this time. Enjoying each other. We showered together. That led to another fuck, quick and hard, with me leaning on the bathroom sink.

We then decided it would be better for us to take a shower separately. As I stood under the falling water, I realised for the first time that his prediction had nearly been right. My pussy wasn't raw. But it had been well-stretched and was a bit sore. It would need a day or two to recover. Not that I was complaining; it had been worth it.

We went down to breakfast separately. Only a few of the wedding guests had stayed the night, and I joined Mum and Dad. I had missed Tony and Catherine leaving for their honeymoon, but nobody seemed to mind. They hadn't made a big exit, just slipped off early. As I ate some toast, I did wonder how Catherine was feeling this morning.

After breakfast, we all went to get ready to leave. I was taking Mum and Dad home, so I waited in the lobby for them to come down. I saw Mike with his friends on the other side of the hall. Then I saw Jane and Anne coming towards me. Jane went straight for it.

"Someone saw Mike leave your room this morning."

"And?" I must have looked over at Mike because I saw him approaching.

"Morning everyone. How are we all this morning?"

Jane and Anne looked at each other, less certain of themselves.

"Morning Mike," I smiled at him. "Apparently, someone saw you leaving my room this morning."

"Did they?" I recognised the glint in his eye; he was thinking of having a bit of fun. I wasn't going to object now. The wedding was over, so I didn't need to be diplomatic.

"Yes," Jane snapped, more certain of herself again. "Whatever were you doing there?"

Mike and I looked at each other, and our eyes agreed on the response.

He leaned towards them confidentially. "Well, girls, if you really want to know …" He looked around, heightening the suspense. "… Mary and I spent the night fucking each other's brains out."

They both visibly recoiled, their faces reddening.

"But if you feel left out, I could fit you in tonight, Jane. And you tomorrow night, Anne. Or I could do you together? You both look like you could do with a good seeing to."

I had to work hard to stifle a laugh. Almost as one, they looked from Mike to me, and back to Mike. Horror and shock on their faces.

Anne recovered first. "I … I wouldn't … I haven't …"

"No, Anne," I said softly. "But perhaps it's about time you did."

This time, it was Mike's turn to cover up a laugh. They looked at each other, and stomped away, carrying their cases towards the door. Mike and I were left standing alone.

"So, Mike. Now you're off to do whatever it is you and your friends do."

"That's about it, Mary. It's been fun."

"Yes, Mike. Quite an experience. Not quite raw … but close enough." I wiggled my hips.

"No complaint, though?"

"Oh no. But I'm not going to get all gushy, either. You might get a big head. And you're quite big enough already."

He leaned across and gave me a quick kiss on the cheek. "Goodbye, Mary. Be good."

"Oh, I always am, Mike."

"Yes, I reckon you are."

Mum and Dad came down at that moment, and Mum walked over to us. Mike turned to greet her. "We're just off, Maureen. We've got a long journey."

Mum smiled. "OK, Mike. Thanks for all your hard work."

He smiled at us both and walked off.

"Mike seems a nice man, dear."

"Yes, he is, Mum."

"It's a pity he's not local; you could get to know one another."

For the second or third time that morning, I had to hide a grin.

"Oh, I'm not sure he's my type, Mum. Ready to go home?"

I never saw Mike again. I asked Tony a couple of times how he was. But I always got an evasive answer and gave up. No, he wasn't my type, but I'll never forget that night.

***

Six months later, we held Dad's funeral at the church where Tony and Catherine were married. Catherine was already pregnant with Sally.

Chapter 4 – The Bad Boy

When I finished college, I found a job in a solicitor's office. It was mundane work, at least to start with, but I was now bringing in some money. Paula had also started work, and we quickly decided to find somewhere to rent, so we could have our own place. In those days, rents were cheaper, and we soon found a two-bedroom flat in a reasonable spot.

We begged and borrowed furniture from our parents, and soon had it set up as best as we could. But for us, it was heaven. A whole stream of guys passed through the flat, rarely staying more than one night.

I wasn't looking for a boyfriend; just a lot of fun. I had a few male friends but liked them to stay just that; friends. When I went out, I still looked past the preening, vain lotharios, looking for their more interesting friends, and it usually worked. But on one occasion, I ended up with a bad boy. So did Paula.

One Saturday night, we went to a club that wasn't on our usual list. We'd heard a lot about it, but it also had a reputation as the place which always ended the evening with a mass brawl. But we thought if we went early, we'd be all right. When we got there, it was very quiet.

Most clubs in the eighties didn't look their best when nearly empty. It was too easy to see how drab and dingy they were. Terrible cheap carpet, more stain than carpet, which stuck to your shoes as you walked over it. And that smell; the same in virtually every club. A mix of stale alcohol, cigarette smoke, sweat, weed and cheap scent. All mixed together with industrial-strength cleaning fluid.

Paula and I had decided to go on our own. Then we could easily leave if we wanted to. But as we sat at a table with our drinks, we wondered if it was even worth staying. A few small groups were dotted around, but nobody was dancing. The music was a weird mix of styles, too. New Romantic, disco, even a bit of punk, but who were they trying to attract? Most of the clubs had a house style; this one couldn't seem to make up its mind. Perhaps music wasn't really its thing. So it proved.

We hung around for a while, and the place gradually started filling up. We didn't see anyone we knew, which was unheard of in the other clubs we frequented. A lot of the clientele seemed to know each other, though, and we were left alone. Although we did attract a lot of furtive – and less than furtive – glances.

We soon realised that a lot of business was going on. Money going one way, little packages going the other. We guessed it was drugs, but the items varied in size, so we were a bit puzzled. In other clubs, weed was commonplace and openly smoked in several. Every few months, the police would carry out a half-hearted raid on one.

Everyone knew the form. If they found you with a few joints or the various nameless pills that got handed round, they'd ignore them. If they found you with enough to sell, they'd cart you off to the station, quietly letting you go a few hours later. If they found heavier stuff, then they would take it seriously, but I hardly ever saw that happen. As we watched, business was brisk, and we couldn't help wondering about it.

After a while, the club settled down and began to look like most other clubs. People started dancing, and people started eyeing each other up and pairing off. We began to see a pattern; there were quite a few girls who found a guy, had a drink with him, perhaps a dance. Then they'd leave. After a while, the girl would be back and repeat the whole thing. We were a bit slow in working out was going on.

"How many do they do in an evening?" Paula asked.

"God knows, let's watch."

We each homed in on a couple of girls and studied them. They all seemed to have it down to a tee. So did the punters. The girl would come in, and as if by magic, a guy would latch on within a minute or two. Most of the guys were older than the usual club crowd; perhaps late twenties, early thirties.

Mind you, some of the girls were of indeterminate age, as well. Drinks would be bought, and the two of them would go off to a table. A few sips, the minimum of conversation, and perhaps a quick boogie. Then they'd leave; drinks always virtually untouched. The girl would be back within half an hour for a repeat performance.

"Forty-five minutes?"

"Yeah, an hour at most."

"So, they started at, what, eight o'clock?"

"Yeah."

"And the club closes at …?"

"Not sure, probably one."

"So that's five or six in an evening."

"Yeah."

We both sat quietly thinking about it.

"I wonder what they charge?" Paula asked.

"Dunno. And I'm not asking."

"No. Nor me. Do you think any of the guys think we're looking for business, too?"

"Oh. I hadn't thought of that."

We both grinned.

"Probably."

"Can we get you ladies anything?"

We were pulled out of our reverie by the question. Standing in front of us were three guys. The one in front was incredibly handsome; tall, muscular, with big jet-black hair. He was wearing tight, black, flecked trousers, with a bolero jacket over a frilly white silk shirt. Sounds awful, now, but then? He looked like he'd stepped out of a music video. I didn't even notice the two guys with him. I looked at Paula; she was rather taken, too. She winked.

"A couple of rum and cokes would be nice," she said sweetly.

The leader raised an arm, and one of the others went off to the bar.

"I'm Stefan," he said, sitting down on my side of the bench. He had a slight accent, but I couldn't place it. "This is Carl, and Ian's off getting the drinks."

"Mary."

"Paula."

"I've not seen you two here before."

"No. We thought we'd see if it deserved its reputation."

"And ...?"

"We were just thinking it probably does."

I looked at him closely. He wasn't my usual type, but there was something about him. He was certainly older than me, but by how much, I couldn't be certain. Yet the air of confidence –

arrogance, almost – was palpable. He seemed in a different league to everyone else in the club.

"Probably," he conceded. "I would be careful if I were you. Some of the girls here are not as … honourable as you seem to be."

"No, we'd worked that out," I said. "How much do they charge?"

Stefan raised an eyebrow and then smiled.

"Looking for a new career?"

"No. Just curious."

"Curiosity can be dangerous." This was said with a certain fierceness, so I took the hint. Luckily, at that moment the third guy returned with the drinks. By this time, Stefan had moved quite close to me, and Carl had attached himself to Paula. Ian hovered on the end of the bench; mostly looking the other way. But Stefan was looking at me; staring straight at me. With a faint smile on his lips. It was slightly unnerving, but it was working. I stared straight back, intrigued by this man.

I normally looked for guys who treated me as an equal; not always easy, but they did exist. I had known from the moment I saw Stefan that he didn't see me as an equal. I was something to conquer, and I began to wonder if I might like being conquered.

"Want to come to a party?" He asked.

"Well, I'm not leaving Paula on her own."

"Oh, she's invited as well. She seems to be getting on with Carl."

I looked over, and they were already very friendly.

"Where is this party?"

"At my house."

"Many people going?"

"No. Just us."

"I see. Paula, what do you think?"

61

She took her eyes off Carl and looked over at me.

"I'm game."

"OK. You're on."

Stefan stood up and held out his hand to help me up. I could feel an edge of danger about him, but it was exciting. He led me towards the entrance, with Carl and Paula following, and Ian bringing up the rear. Outside, we waited while Ian wandered off.

"He's just getting the car," Stefan said.

Ian returned driving a large, black Mercedes, and we all piled in. Paula was sitting on Carl's lap, and they already had their hands under clothing. Stefan and I sat squashed next to one another, but not saying much. I could feel his thigh next to mine, and he gently rested his hand on my leg. My skirt was short, so his hand was on my bare skin. I looked down and saw a ring on each finger; they weren't costume jewellery either.

I didn't really watch where we were going, which was probably stupid, but after about fifteen minutes, we pulled into a driveway, and the car stopped. Ian got out and opened the door on Stefan's side, and he helped me out. We were standing in front of a large house; not grand but surrounded by a tall wall. I looked over at Paula; she just shrugged and squealed. I think Carl's hand was responsible for that.

"Come," Stefan said. He followed Ian towards the front door. It was clear Ian was the general flunkey. He hadn't said a word so far. We went into the hallway, and Ian duly went around turning on the lights, pulling curtains, and Stefan ushered us into a large room. Obviously, the main room in the house. It was achingly modern. Leather sofas, bright rugs, black and steel furniture.

"Drink? Another rum and coke?"

"Thanks. Yes."

As I expected, Ian went over to the bar in the corner of the room and got to work. Stefan waved his hand at a sofa, and I sat down. Taking off his jacket, he settled alongside.

"So why were you at the club tonight?" He asked.

"We're out every Saturday night somewhere. Just tried a different venue tonight."

"Will you be coming again?"

"I doubt it; it's not really our scene."

Stefan laughed.

"No, I think it's a bit ... dangerous for you and your friend."

"Oh, I don't mind a bit of excitement."

He was toying with me. As Ian brought our drinks over, I watched Stefan. He was still completely in charge. Cool as a cucumber. Mildly amused by the situation, I think.

"And what were you doing there?" I asked him. His face took on a harder look momentarily, then softened again.

"Oh, a mix of business and pleasure."

"Business?"

"I never discuss my business with people I don't know." That meaner look again.

"OK, I can take a hint."

"Good. It's for the best."

I was intrigued, and a little scared. This situation was a bit heavy. Here was a guy of maybe thirty, with a house way beyond most people's means. He wasn't selling burgers, that was certain.

"You want a joint? Or something harder?" He asked.

"A joint is my limit, but I wouldn't mind one."

Ian immediately brought some over and took some over to Carl and Paula. Looking over, I saw that they were already way ahead of us. Hands all over each other and Carl's hand was exploring inside Paula's blouse.

Stefan lit a joint and handed it to me. I took a slow puff. I was getting better at judging strength now, so wanted to be careful.

"Don't worry; it's just normal stuff," Stefan said.

"Just checking," I replied. "Can't allow myself to fall into the wrong hands."

"Looks like your friend is in the right hands."

I looked over again, and Paula now had her hand in Carl's undone trousers, obviously stroking his dick. His hand was between her spread legs, and they were kissing furiously. As we watched, she pushed his trousers down to his knees and pulled his dick free from his boxers. Without a break, she bent down and covered the head with her mouth.

Although we had shared a room at her parent's house, we had put a curtain up between our beds. We had caught glimpses of each other's activities if we'd had to go out to the bathroom, but this was the first time we'd been quite so brazen. I quickly realised that I was really turned on. Watching other people having sex was a new experience, and it was exciting. Stefan brought me back to the present.

"So, you want to watch? Or you want to fuck?"

"Can't we do both?" I asked.

"You may not be a working girl, but somehow I don't think you're an innocent, either."

"Would I have come here if I was?"

"No, I guess not. So, what's it to be?"

"Why did you invite us?"

We were teasing each other. But it was really turning me on. And I couldn't help seeing Paula and Carl getting it on. I only wanted one thing. He looked straight at me.

"Her," he said, motioning towards Paula, "because she was with you, and Carl seems to like her. You, because you're going to suck my dick, and then I'm going to fuck you."

"Very sure of yourself, aren't you?"

"Yes. I'm normally right."

"What if I say no?"

"Then Ian will take you home. But you're not, are you?"

"Oh no."

I got up and stood in front of him. With indecent haste, I stripped off everything I was wearing.

"Way to go, girl!" Paula said, rather loudly from the other side of the room. I looked around, as she followed suit, standing up, and removing what clothes she was still wearing, before kneeling between Carl's legs again.

I bent down, and undid Stefan's trousers, pulling them down. He unbuttoned his shirt and took it off, leaving him in a pair of boxers.

"Well, those have got to come off as well," I said, before grabbing the waistband. He lifted himself up, as I pulled them down, revealing his hard dick. Nothing special, but circumcised. That was a first for me. It certainly looked different. I knelt between his legs, rested my arms on his legs, and started to stroke his dick and balls. With no foreskin, I was a little baffled about the best way to tease him. So, I just decided to get to work with my mouth.

I was feeling horny and I could hear little moans and cries from the other sofa, which really added to the atmosphere. As I sucked him, he stroked my hair, and once or twice, held my head still on his dick. I surreptitiously moved one hand back between my legs and started playing with myself. I got the impression that my pleasure wasn't high on Stefan's agenda. He didn't say anything but seemed to be enjoying what I was doing.

So was I, and I quickly brought myself to orgasm. As I did, he grabbed my arm and pushed me onto the floor. Following me down, he turned me around and pulled me up onto my hands and knees. In front of me, I saw Carl and Paula. He was still sitting on the sofa, naked, and Paula was straddling him, riding his dick. Before I took in the whole scene, Stefan slid his into my pussy and started roughly fucking me.

It was a bit surreal really. Here I was, on all fours, being screwed, watching my best friend, not six feet away, bouncing up and down on another guy. It was horny, and I felt myself building up to orgasm again. But it didn't come, Stefan did. Groaning as he did so, then pulling out quite abruptly, and giving my bum a slap.

I thought about carrying on myself but thought better of it. Dropping to the carpet, I looked around and saw Stefan's face. The mask seemed to have slipped. His face was almost angry; tight, veined. For the first time in the evening, I felt a shudder of fear. But his face soon softened again. Just as the groans from the other side of the room told us that they'd finished too. Well, Carl had. I hadn't heard Paula come to orgasm, and I knew her sounds quite well by now. They flopped down, recovering.

"Well," Stefan said, "that's better. We're all happy now."

"More relaxed, certainly," I replied. "Where's the loo?"

Paula and I went to clean up.

"You were keen tonight," I said in the bathroom.

"You weren't exactly shy."

"True. Was Carl any good?"

"Keen enough, but only for himself. Stefan?"

"Yeah, the same."

"Bloody typical."

When we got back, Ian had replenished our drinks. I think we'd forgotten about him, but I realised he'd been in the room the whole time. More joints were lit, and we sat there on the floor, passing them around. Not much was said. I noticed that

66

Stefan and Carl took very shallow draws, possibly not really inhaling at all, so I was careful not to get too stoned either. After a while, Carl started stroking Paula again.

"Want to swap?" Stefan asked, looking at me, then at Carl. I looked at Paula; she shrugged slightly.

"OK," I said. So, I crawled over to Carl, and Paula switched to Stefan. The second round was less frantic, and a bit mechanical. These guys only seemed to know two sexual acts. Girl sucks dick; guy fucks girl. That's exactly what happened. The one saving grace for me was that doing this while watching what Paula was doing was horny enough for me to reach orgasm again.

As we recovered, the phone rang, and Ian answered it. He handed it to Stefan, who had a very brief conversation, consisting mainly of 'yes' or 'no'. When he handed it back to Ian, he turned to us.

"Well, ladies. I'm sorry, but the party is over. I have things to do. Ian will take you home."

It wasn't an offer; more a command. We gathered our clothes and got dressed.

"Thanks for coming," Stefan said. "If you want to party again, I'm in the club most Saturday evenings; some Friday's as well. And if you're looking for a career change, let me know."

"Thanks, Stefan. It's a bit out of our usual patch, but who knows?"

"Who indeed. Just tell Ian where you want to go."

With that we were dismissed, Ian leading us to the front door. As we walked over to the car, Paula came close.

"Don't give him our address."

"I wasn't going to; I had the same thought. Taxi rank?"

"Yeah."

The drive back into town was silent. Ian – who still had not said a word all evening – dropped us at the taxi rank. We waited for a few minutes after he'd left and got a taxi home. We never went to that club again, and although I did see Stefan around a few times, we didn't acknowledge one another. I doubt he even remembered me.

Chapter 5 – The Cheat

I now found the job which I've done, on and off, ever since. I became a trainee Barrister's Clerk. At the time, it was unusual for a woman. It was a bit of a closed world anyway. But one of the solicitors where I worked could see I was bored, so when a friend of his mentioned that her chambers were looking for a new clerk, he recommended me.

I went for three interviews before I was taken on. I found out later that my youth and sex counted heavily against me. But Helena – the barrister friend of my solicitor – had pushed hard, and they finally took me on for a trial period. I can say, with all due modesty, that I repaid her faith over the next few years.

The amount of work came as a bit of a shock, compared to the boredom of the solicitor's office. I had so much to learn, and fast. Not only the mechanics of the job, but also how barristers worked, how the courts worked, and lots of stuff about the legal system in general. There were lots of long nights of reading and study.

Seven barristers worked out of the chambers; Helena was the only woman. Then there was Henry, the senior clerk, Patrick, the junior clerk, and me. Very much the trainee. It took me a long time to prove myself to Henry, but I got on well with Patrick, as you'll see.

All this hard work was interesting, but there was still plenty of time for fun. Some things had changed, though. I was no longer sharing with Paula. We hadn't fallen out; she'd found herself a husband. Well, he wasn't initially, obviously, but he was later. Chris; nice enough guy. They quickly decided they wanted to live together, and I offered to move out, so he could move in.

I found a small flat quite close to the chambers and set myself up as a single girl; I loved it. I'd enjoyed sharing with Paula, but I soon relished living on my own. No-one to depend on, no-one to complain about dirty knickers lying on the floor. It set the pattern for my life ever since.

With Paula now occupied elsewhere, I didn't have a partner in crime for Saturday nights anymore. We still met up, but usually with Chris, and the evenings were much less chaotic. I did have other friends, but we weren't as close. The girls seemed to be solely looking for husbands, and the guys were looking for steady girlfriends. I found all this a bit boring. Was I growing up? Perhaps they were and leaving me behind. But I was very quiet for a few months on the man front. The world I was working in was overwhelmingly male, but they were mostly all much older than me, so that was no good. Then I met Tom.

I was sitting on a bench in a corridor in the County Court building. Helena was in court, and I had some papers to give her before the next session in the afternoon. Sitting on the other end of the bench was a man engrossed in some paperwork. I guessed he was in the same position as me; waiting to speak to his barrister. He finally put the bundle of papers down and looked in my direction.

"Morning," he said.

"Hello."

"Are you the girl clerk at Cross Street?"

"Am I famous already?"

"Sort of. It's been the talk of our chambers."

"Don't tell me; it would never happen there."

"Something like that."

"You're a clerk as well?"

"Yeah."

"How would you feel about a female clerk working with you?"

"Wouldn't bother me; as long as they can do the job. I've been in three different chambers. I left one because the senior clerk was virtually senile; absolutely useless. Mind you, seniors can be a race apart."

"Yes."

"How are you getting on with Henry?"

"Good question. Well, he does speak to me now, rather than just ignoring me, so I think that's progress."

The courtroom doors opened, and people started coming out.

"I'm Tom, by the way. I guess we're likely to meet here quite often."

"Probably. I'm Mary."

Helena appeared at the doorway, saw me, and came over to the bench. I spent a few minutes passing over the papers, before heading back to chambers. When she returned from court at the end of the day, she stopped at my desk.

"I see you've met Tom." She had a curious smile on her face.

"Yes. Apparently, I'm the talk of his chambers."

"I don't doubt it. Just warning you that he has something of a reputation."

"How do you know I don't?"

She smiled.

"I don't care about any reputation you might have outside work. But I want you to build a damned good reputation for what you do here. Even Henry was complimentary about you the other day, weren't you Henry?"

There was a mumbled harrumph from behind the piles of papers which permanently obscured Henry's desk at the far end of the room.

"So, you must be doing something right."

She leaned closer.

"I know how hard it still is for a woman in all this. Rightly or wrongly, we're judged more harshly than men. Don't become a nun; God knows, I'm not, but just remember that."

That evening at home, I thought about what Helena had said. She was right. I knew many girls who had reputations. Still surprised that I didn't seem to because I couldn't see they'd done more than Paula and I had. Guys, of course, would have the same reputation. But for them it was positive; for the girls, it definitely wasn't. It was unfair but real enough.

I also realised that I had changed. The clubbing days seemed to be in the past; when I did go out on Saturday night, I didn't enjoy it as much. On one occasion, it hit me that most of the clubbers were now a few years younger than me. I suddenly felt old!

The following week, I bumped into Tom in the same corridor. This time we started chatting straight away. I couldn't help studying him; now I knew he had a reputation. That made him more interesting to me. But at first, I couldn't see anything special about him. He was pleasant enough, talked easily, and listened. Not especially good-looking, but smart and well-groomed.

"Fancy grabbing lunch?"

"Uh, sorry?" I realised I'd missed the last few sentences.

"Fancy grabbing lunch? The Flag around the corner is good and service is quick."

I checked the time; nearly lunchtime.

"Yes, OK. But I've only got about half an hour."

The bar was full, but we ordered and managed to find the end of a table to perch on.

"How are you getting on?" He asked.

"OK, I think. Apparently, even Henry is happy."

"Oh, well. You've cracked it then."

We chatted for a while about work as we ate lunch. His view of good food clearly wasn't mine, as the Chilli was awful. But it filled a hole.

"Got a boyfriend?" He asked.

"No."

"I'm surprised."

"What if I don't want one?"

"Lesbian?"

"You're bold."

"Perhaps."

"And no, I'm not into women. I just grab some fun when I want it. Not looking to get tied down."

"Ah, a girl after my own heart."

"I'm told you have a reputation."

He looked at me.

"Do I?"

"Apparently."

"Want to find out if it's true?"

"I might."

"How about Friday night; meet you here at seven. I'll find somewhere for dinner."

It was all a bit unexpected, but what the hell.

"Yeah. OK."

It was my first proper date for some time, so I spent a while getting ready. A bath, and a careful choice of clothes. I found I was looking forward to it. In the past, it had been a case of putting something on to attract attention, going to a club, and picking from the moths attracted to the light. Tonight, that wasn't the case. It was actually scarier. Just him and me.

I got to the Flag just after seven – a girl never arrives on time, let alone early. It's not presumption; it just means that your date should already be there, and you don't have to enter alone or put up with unwanted attention. Tom was standing at the bar, waiting.

"Hello, Mary. You look good."

"Hi, Tom. Thanks."

I'd chosen a rather tight dress with padded shoulders, and a low neckline. Long enough on the leg to hide my stocking tops. I'd spent some time bigging up my hair. Mind you, he looked good too. A light grey suit with tiny black flecks all through it, a white shirt with a skinny tie, and grey winkle-pickers. His hair was slicked down, and he had an earring in his left ear.

"You don't look so bad, either."

"Well, I've got to live up to my reputation. Drink?"

"Uh, yes. Campari and Soda, please."

He caught the barmaid's attention, and we took our drinks over to a table.

"I've got a table booked for dinner at seven-thirty at the Berni. It's only a few minutes' walk."

"Mmm, fine."

Twenty minutes later, we were shown to our table in the restaurant. The Berni Inn was something of a British institution. Mocked by many, it was still very popular, and I was ambivalent about it. I was interested that Tom had brought me here. Was it because this was his style, or because it was anonymous?

I decided to go with the flow and have what was known as the 'Great British Meal' at the time. Prawn Cocktail, Steak and Black Forest Gateau. It was what the chain was famous for.

"What fun have you grabbed lately, then?" Tom asked.

"Not much. I've been busy reading lots of the books Patrick has lent me."

"It's got to be done, but you must have some downtime, as well."

"Yeah, but it's taken a bit of a back seat. I'm living on my own now that my old flatmate got hitched. She was always my partner in crime."

"Crime?"

"Oh, you know. Saturday nights on the town."

"On the town, or on the pull?"

I shrugged.

"Mostly the latter."

"I suspect you were mostly successful."

"What makes you say that?"

He leaned back in his seat.

"Come on, Mary, don't be shy. You're pretty, and you know it. You're confident, and you know it. In most clubs around here, you'd have had the pick of the guys."

"Yeah, OK. I admit it. I was a bit wild."

"Different guy every night?"

I laughed.

"Do you normally insult your dates?"

"Oh, I'm not judging. I was the same, only less successful, I suspect. You said was?"

"I seem to have changed recently. I don't really go clubbing anymore, I'm fed up with being part of the cattle market."

"But still want some fun?"

"Oh yes."

As the meal progressed, I decided I liked Tom. He was cheeky, but not trying too hard. Every so often, he'd drop in an unexpected question or comment, and it kept me on my toes. I started to relax and match his cheek.

"So, if you didn't manage a different girl every night, how often did you score?" I asked him.

"Every two or three weeks, I suppose. I went around with a couple of other guys then, and both were better looking than me. They often got the pick. If we matched up with two or three girls, then …well."

"You missed out or had to make do with the wallflower?"

"Something like that. But sometimes it worked to my advantage. The wallflower was often a bit of a dark horse."

"Yeah, well. It's always worth having a few hidden skills."

"And what are yours?"

"If I told you, they wouldn't be hidden, would they?"

"Now you're teasing."

"Yes, that's a skill I don't hide."

"So how does a guy get to discover the hidden ones?"

"Depends if I like him or not."

"Do you like me?"

"I'm beginning to."

I was. I was having fun. Our chat was light, with plenty of banter, and he wasn't patronising me or trying too hard. If this was him being natural, great. If this was the style that got him his reputation, I still wasn't going to object. I'd not had sex for a few weeks, and I decided to end that drought.

We'd finished eating and had ordered snowballs. While we waited, I quietly took a shoe off, and casually laid my foot on his under the table. We continued talking; I saw no reaction from him, so slowly ran my foot up his leg. His demeanour was still unchanged. But he finally jumped slightly as my foot landed on the seat and settled between his legs. Pushing my toes forward, I could feel his stiff dick through his trousers.

"I thought I was the one with the reputation," he said.

"Perhaps I want to test it."

"I can see that."

"Want me to stop?"

"No, but we could move on somewhere."

"In a hurry?

"Yes. No." He frowned. "I think you're winning this little competition."

"What competition is that?"

"You're dangerous."

"Me? No. You're the one with the reputation."

"I think the tables have turned tonight. Perhaps I should surrender now."

"Oh, don't be a spoilsport. I've only just begun."

I had now managed to push his dick so it was pointing up and was rubbing my foot up and down over his balls as well. He was clearly enjoying it, but I could see the frustration on his face. He couldn't really do anything in return. It wasn't so easy for him to take a shoe off, and he was smart enough to know that I probably wouldn't welcome the tip of a winkle-picker between my thighs.

"We could find a hotel," he said. "My place is quite a distance."

"Mine's a five-minute walk."

He called the waiter over and asked for the bill, which he paid as soon as it arrived.

"Shall we?" He asked.

"Why not?"

I retrieved my foot and slipped my shoe back on. Standing up, I waited while he rearranged himself, trying not to allow his bulge to show too obviously. I was aware that I wanted him. My flat suddenly seemed a long way away. Outside the restaurant, I turned to him and gave him a long kiss. He responded and pulled me in close to him, placing a hand on my bum, and caressing it. I put a hand on his crotch and squeezed.

"Behave; at least for the next five minutes."

"And then?"

"We'll see."

We walked quickly, both wanting to shorten that five minutes. I led him to the door of my block and let us into the hallway. Once inside, he grabbed me, turned me around to face him, and started to kiss me passionately. His hand grabbed my bum again. This time, I didn't stop him, and he lifted my dress until he found the top of my stocking. Just as he touched my naked thigh, I pulled his hand away.

"I want you," he whispered.

"When we get upstairs, you can have me."

We climbed the stairs two or three at a time. I opened my front door and turned the light on. Tom shut the door behind him and pushed me against the wall. We both wanted it. He kissed me hard, running his hands up and down my body. I responded and pushed his jacket off his shoulders. Undoing his tie, I almost ripped his shirt off.

He'd lifted the hem of my dress up above my waist now, and his hand went straight to my pussy, rubbing through my briefs. I

78

reached down and undid his trousers, letting them drop to the floor, and slid his boxers down. Finally grabbing his dick, eliciting a groan as I did so.

I pushed him away slightly, grabbed the hem of my dress and pulled it over my head. He pushed me against the wall again, and his dick pressed into my crotch.

"Do I need a johnny?" He asked.

"No."

That was the invitation he needed.

"Turn around."

I faced the wall, and he pulled me back, so I was leaning against it with my bum sticking out. He pulled my briefs down, and ran a finger between my legs, I opened them, but my knickers were still around my thighs, so they didn't open far. It didn't deter him. I felt his dick at the entrance to my pussy and gasped as he slid it in.

We were both worked up, and he started to screw me with long, regular strokes. His hand moved to my clit, and he played with it, rubbing it between his fingers. It wasn't long before I was close to orgasm, and when I came, my legs started to shake, and I had to struggle to maintain my position. Tom sensed it and paused.

I pulled forward, so he slipped out, and turned around. He looked at me quizzically. I grabbed his dick.

"Let's go somewhere more comfortable."

Guiding him by his dick, I led him into the living room, put the light on as we went in, and led him towards the sofa. I let go of him and finally took my bra and knickers off.

"Now, where were we?"

I knelt in front of him and took the head of his dick into my mouth, using my hands to play with his balls. He groaned again. I'd come, he hadn't, but I knew he needed to. I wondered how long he'd let me have control. Not long, it turned out. He pulled away and drew me up. Giving me a strong kiss, he pushed me back until the backs of my legs hit the sofa. He pushed me down on it and knelt between my legs.

Spreading them, he guided his dick back into me. Placing a hand either side of me on the sofa, he started to screw me; harder this time. Occasionally bending forward to kiss me. I felt myself growing to orgasm again, and just relaxed, letting it all happen. I came abruptly, and as I did so, Tom came as well, his spasms conflicting with mine.

He slowly collapsed onto me, and we lay there, recovering. After a while, I heard him laugh quietly.

"What?"

"I'll admit, I set out to have you tonight. But I think it may have been you that's had me."

"Does it matter?"

He looked at me with a sly smile.

"But what about my reputation?"

"Your secret's safe with me."

We both grinned, and he lifted himself off me. When we'd both been to the bathroom, I got us a drink, and we sat on the floor. He stayed the night, but we didn't get much sleep. Whatever his supposed reputation was for, he turned out to be a good lover, and when he left in the morning, I was very relaxed and happy.

I met up with Tom a few times over the following weeks; in addition to when we met in the court buildings. But he never stayed the night again; there was always some excuse, which I began to think odd. Then I found out why.

One Saturday afternoon, I was walking through town doing a bit of window shopping. As I turned away from one shop, I came face to face with a typical family group. Except the man was Tom. I saw a flash of panic cross his face, as I decided what to do. I could acknowledge him or ignore him. He decided for me.

"Hello, Mary."

"Hi, Tom."

There was an awkward moment's silence.

"Uh, this is Hilary. Hil, this is Mary, the new clerk at Cross Street."

Hilary looked at me for a moment.

"Hello Mary, I've heard all about you."

I doubted that, but I wasn't going to make a big thing of this. "Hello."

"And this is Mark." He nodded to a lad of about five. "And Katie." This to a tot in a pushchair.

"Hello," I said to both or either of them. But I got no response. Mark hid behind his father's legs, and Katie just gave me a bored stare.

The awkwardness returned, so I broke it this time.

"Nice to meet you Hilary, but I must go. I'm meeting someone."

"Yes, nice to meet you too."

And with that, I was gone. Well. That explained the excuses.

The next week, I was sitting on the bench outside court number three again and saw Tom come into the corridor. He stopped, and just stood there.

"Oh, come on Tom. I'm not going to bite."

He walked cautiously over to the bench.

"Thanks," he said.

"What for?"

"Not making a scene."

"No point in that. People might get hurt. Particularly children."

"Yeah."

"Strictly professional relationship from now on Tom."

"I guess so."

Helena went past my desk later that day.

"Helena?"

"Yes, Mary."

"You know Tom?"

"Yes."

"And his reputation."

"Yes."

"It's all true."

She gave me a quizzical look, but I wasn't saying anything more, so she smiled, and walked on.

Chapter 6 – My Friend Patrick

Patrick and I had become friends very quickly after I started working with him. The office was small, and a bit isolated. On a day to day basis, we didn't spend much time with the barristers; they were either in their offices or in court. The only other person around was the ever-present Henry.

Without Patrick's help, I would have floundered within days. He patiently taught me everything I needed to know over my first few months, and never criticised or got angry. I will be forever grateful to him for that.

At first, I couldn't quite work him out, though. He was quiet, almost shy, but had an easy manner with everyone. He told me later that he was glad to have someone else in the office. Being there with just Henry for company had been something of a chore.

Henry was the mainstay of the clerk's office; indeed, of the chambers. He'd been there since the year dot, knew everything and everyone, and, for all his grumpiness and remoteness, was incredibly efficient. But worried about a happy and inclusive office environment, he was not. My arrival meant that Patrick finally had someone to talk to and share the load with.

Pat was a small man, not more than about 5'6", with a lean build, and wiry frame. At first, I couldn't place his accent, but I learned he was from an Irish family who had moved to Liverpool when he was small, and it clicked into place. He didn't talk much about his family, except in a very abstract way, and he never discussed his private life. Even Henry occasionally talked about his wife and children, if only to moan about them; but Patrick kept quiet.

I wouldn't have called him handsome, but he had a certain charisma about him and a real twinkle in his eye. I don't think I ever saw him glum or morose. Perhaps in the arrogance of my youth, I began to wonder why he never tried flirting with me.

One Friday evening, I was putting things away at the end of the day. Henry left us to shut the office down.

"All ready, Pat?" I asked.

"Oh, you can go, I'll shut up."

"OK. You still got stuff to do?"

"Uh, no. I've got something arranged for tonight, but it's not until 8ish, so I'll stay here until then."

"Are you sure? I live a couple of streets away. Come around, and I'll get us something to eat. Be comfier than sitting here for three hours."

He thought for a moment or two; I thought he was weighing me up in some way.

"If you're sure I'm not disturbing you, Mary."

"No, nothing planned for tonight," I replied, "unfortunately."

We turned out the lights, checked no-one was left in the building and locked up. Within a few minutes, we reached my flat.

"God, you are close to the office, aren't you? I live about forty-five minutes away, so it's pretty pointless going home and coming back in later."

"Got something special planned?"

"Just a night out."

"Sounds good," I replied, going into my bedroom. "Make yourself at home, I'm just going to change quickly. There's beer in the fridge or wine somewhere in the kitchen. Help yourself."

"Thanks."

When I got back to the kitchen, he was leaning against the worktop, beer in hand, looking out of the window.

"Fancy something to eat? I'm not a great cook, but I can turn my hand to the basics."

"That would be good; I was going to get a takeaway somewhere, so anything will be better than that."

"Wait until you've eaten it first."

I looked in the fridge, not having planned on a guest this evening. There wasn't much there.

"Well, it looks like an omelette with whatever I've got in here. Hope that's OK."

I set about emptying the fridge and found a few mushrooms, some onions, cheese, and the remains of some ham. It would have to do.

"Do you live here alone?" He asked.

"Yes, I used to share with a friend, but she got engaged, so I moved out to give them space. Luckily, I found this place; suits me fine."

"I wasn't even aware anybody lived around here; I thought it was all businesses."

"I know, I didn't either. But there are quite a few flats over the shops and offices. I'm getting to know a few of my neighbours."

"No boyfriend?"

"Not at the moment. Why? You applying?"

He gave me a curious look.

"Hardly, Mary."

I turned towards him.

"I'm not your type, eh?"

He looked at me thoughtfully for a while. A faint smile crossed his face before he finally replied.

"Well, you're the wrong sex, for a start."

After a slight pause, I burst out laughing. His smile broadened.

"Oh, sorry, Pat. I hadn't twigged."

"No reason you should have. I don't exactly advertise it. Not at work, anyway."

"I guess not. I must admit, I put on my 'good girl' look for the office."

"Meaning you're not really a good girl?"

"What was it Mae West said? 'When I'm good, I'm very, very good, but when I'm bad, I'm better'?"

"Ooh, is there more to you than I know then, Mary?"

"We all seem to have our secrets, Pat."

"Touché!"

I put together a reasonable meal, and we sat down to eat.

"Dare I ask what you're up to tonight then, Pat?"

"Oh, just meeting up with a couple of friends, and cruising."

"Cruising? Do you mean you're on the pull?

He grinned.

"Maybe."

"Sorry, that was a rude question. I'm far from innocent, but I admit I don't know anything about the ... I don't even know what the right term is ... queer scene?"

"That's as good a term as any."

"I guess I'm just curious."

He gave a mischievous grin.

"About being queer, or about the scene?"

"Just about the scene … I think."

"I imagine it's not much different really, just a little more discreet. Until you find the right place; then you can let your hair down."

"So, where's the right place around here?"

"If I told you, I'd have to kill you! There are two or three places that are well-known and safe. Perhaps I'll show you sometime."

"That might be fun, but would I be welcome?"

"Oh God, yeah. Queer people are generally more accepting of straights than the other way around."

I was curious; Pat's world was one that I obviously knew existed, but had had little contact with; at least, knowingly. After that night, Pat often used my flat as a stopping-off point for his nights out. A few weeks later, he took me along to meet his friends. We got on well from the beginning. I was – ignorantly – surprised that it included both men and women.

I suppose I'd thought that gay men would stick together, and gay women would do the same. But the group was a wonderful mix of people, and, looking back, with almost all the 80s stereotypes of gay people represented. Butch men, camp men, butch girls, feminine girls, an occasional cross-dresser.

And on several occasions, an elderly male couple, who had been together for over forty years, and had suffered badly prior to decriminalisation. They were respected by everyone and rather enjoyed the notoriety; and the steady supply of drinks that came their way.

I went out regularly with the group. I did get quite a lot of offers, all of which I declined politely. Looking back, perhaps I should have accepted at least one.

Chapter 7 – An Interesting Holiday

The following year, Pat and I decided to go skiing. God knows why; neither of us had done it before, but we set our minds on it. We had a bit of trouble arranging to take time off from chambers at the same time, but eventually, it was agreed. We booked with a group to go to a resort on the French/Swiss border, who's name I can no longer even remember. I may not remember much about the place, or the skiing, but it's a holiday I will never forget for quite another reason.

This was well before the era of cheap flights, so getting there involved a twenty-four-hour trip in a rather basic coach with no toilet, and a rough ferry crossing. But we knew no different; it all added to the experience. Most of the group were between twenty and thirty, and we soon found that we weren't the only ones who hadn't been skiing before. We relaxed and determined to enjoy ourselves.

On arriving at the resort, we found ourselves allocated to a couple of chalets. When I say chalet, don't imagine a grand wooden building on a high mountain slope, with huge panoramic windows and roaring fires, as depicted in so many movies. These were functional at best; wooden, warm and cosy, yes. But not exactly luxurious. At least each had a resident member of staff to look after us.

'Chalet Girl' was one of the icons of the eighties. They were virtually all girls and came almost exclusively from the upper-middle and upper classes. They did the job for next to nothing (probably didn't need the money) but in return got a couple of weeks at the end of their stint to ski for free. They did the cleaning and the cooking, which turned out to be of the basic, but acceptable, kind.

We were left to sort out our own room arrangements. Some of the party were couples, but there were several small groups of friends, and they had to decide who was going to share with who. Although Pat and I weren't a couple, we quickly agreed to share a room.

"Well, Mary, I'd rather share with someone I know, than someone I don't. But it's a lot to ask of you."

"Oh, I don't mind, Pat. As long as you promise to look the other way when I get undressed."

"I promise. But don't worry, I think it's too late to straighten me out."

We ended up in a reasonable room; two single beds, a wardrobe, two chairs, and a table. The bathroom was across the landing, which seemed convenient, but we hadn't considered all the late-night comings and goings as people visited it on their drunken way in every evening.

Next morning, we went to pick up our equipment. For those of us new to skiing, this was a source of much hilarity and not a little fear. Trying on boots, gloves, skis, salopettes, hats, and everything else we'd need. The staff were as patient as saints; no doubt used to a bunch of new idiots every week. This week, it happened to be us.

When we were all kitted out, we were asked our experience levels. Those who had skied before went off to have fun. We beginners were introduced to our two instructors; Gilles and Armand. I can't really remember much about the lessons, but there was lots of stuff about leaning your body into turns and bending your knees.

When they thought we could at least all stand upright, they moved us over to the nursery slopes, and let us loose. This resort was clearly aimed at less-experienced visitors; there were a lot of practice slopes and easy runs. All of them pretty gentle. There were some higher ones for the skilled, but I don't think there were many black runs nearby.

Which was lucky, because both Pat and I turned out to be utterly useless. I could set off in a straight line but struggled to turn at all. I rapidly got the nickname 'bowling ball' because once I had set off, that was it. Rather than going around anything or anyone in my way, I just went through them or into them. The rest of the group soon learned to get out of my way. Others weren't so lucky, and I don't think I've said 'sorry' so much in one week, before or since.

As for Pat, well, he soon became the group clown; not altogether deliberately, but he did take it in good grace. He had trouble just staying upright at first. Once he had mastered that, he fell over as soon as he tried to move. Armand spent a couple of hours with him, helping him to build his confidence, and after that, he could at least ski around the lower ends of the practice slopes without falling over too often.

At the end of the day, we went back to the chalets; most of us exhausted. All of us with aching knees and hips, bruised bums; someone with a black eye (I never worked out how). We went to our rooms to change for the evening. Pat and I weren't shy about wandering around in our underwear, and we took the opportunity to have a lie-down.

"God, my bum hurts," Pat said, after a while. I burst out laughing; he grinned. "Not that way. That's a piece of cake compared to skiing."

An hour later, we met up for dinner; plain, but filling, with plenty of cheap plonk. Our chalet girl, Clarissa, was nice enough. She proved efficient, without being very helpful, and probably looked down on us from the heights of privilege. But one thing she did seem to know was where the best bars and clubs were. Over dinner, she gave us a quick rundown of the nightlife in the town.

That first night, we went out as one big group to get the feel of the place, going from one bar to the next, then trying the clubs. Clarissa's descriptions turned out to be largely accurate, although the places she had praised the most were a bit expensive.

The next day was spent improving our skills on the slopes. Even though I was hopeless, I was enjoying it, and Pat was still seeing the funny side. In the afternoon, we chose not to ski, but to have a go at skating. Admittedly, if we couldn't master balance on skis, we weren't likely to be any better on skates, but it seemed silly not to try.

There were several rinks around the town; a couple indoors, and a few just open-air. We went to one near our chalet and hired some skates. When we reached the ice, we realised our first mistake. Because it was outside, there was no rail around the edge, so nothing to hold on to for balance. We gingerly put one skate on the ice and held each other's hand before launching ourselves forward; and promptly landing in a heap.

We crawled back to the edge and sat down. Then our saviours – and our shame – arrived. We looked up, and three children, no more than eight or nine were standing in front of us. Two boys and a girl. One of the boys held out his hand and I grabbed it. The other grabbed Pat's hand, and they helped us up. The girl held our other hands between us, and they led us back on to the ice.

The difference was immediately apparent. Although we still struggled, the kids had a steadying effect, and we slowly skated around in a long line. In the next half an hour or so, we made real progress, and after a while, the children let go, and we were able to carry on without them.

Well, admittedly with a few falls. We gave them a few francs each, and they raced off to offer their help to other helpless visitors. I reckon they were onto a nice little earner, but it had been worth it. We skated a couple more times before we left.

On the third night, I struck lucky. Pat had decided not to go out; he'd got very cold during the day, and was feeling a bit fragile, so he stayed in the chalet, and I went out with one of the other girls. We went to one of the clubs which seemed to cater as much for the locals as tourists; always a good sign.

It turned out to be the place where most of the instructors and chalet girls went in their downtime. After a couple of drinks, my companion got chatting to a guy, and I felt a little on my own.

"May I join you?" I looked up, and it was Armand, one of our instructors. "Mary, isn't it?"

"Yes, of course, Armand."

He sat down and put a bottle and two small glasses on the table.

"A drink?"

I smiled to myself. His technique was clearly direct; no doubt refined to precision.

"Thank you. What is it?"

He opened the bottle and filled both glasses to the brim.

"It's called obstler. It's from Alsace, like schnapps, only French. You have to drink it in one go."

I laughed. "I've heard about guys like you."

"I think you probably have." Smiling, he lifted his glass, and downed it in one, replacing it on the table with a gentle bang. He then watched me; challenging me to follow suit. I picked up the bottle and looked at the label. My French wasn't very good, but it did say 'obstler' and 'Alsace', so that was a start.

I put it down, picked up the glass, and sniffed it. A strong, fruity smell accosted me, along with a strong hint of alcohol. I had no idea how strong it was, but I knew Schnapps could be potent stuff. But I was not exactly unaccustomed to alcohol, so decided to risk it. Placing it to my lips, I tipped the glass and emptied it.

An intense heat hit the back of my throat, and I coughed involuntarily but controlled it. The alcohol rapidly spread through me; I'd have to be careful. I banged the glass down on the table and looked at him.

He grinned. "Bravo." As he rapidly refilled both glasses, I was very glad we'd had a good, filling meal before we came out.

I had noticed Armand; most of the women in the group had. He was tall, muscular and confident. Dark hair, blue eyes, with a twinkle to them. I thought he must have a ball working here.

"Your boyfriend is not here?"

I was puzzled for an instant. "Oh, Pat. No, he's just a friend. We both wanted to try skiing, so decided to book together."

"Perhaps he just wants to be your boyfriend."

"Oh, no. A girlfriend is one thing he's not looking for."

He gave me a quizzical look, which quickly broke into a knowing grin.

"Ah, he's out looking for a boyfriend."

Realising I might have said too much, I moved to change the subject.

"Your English is very good."

"Thank you. I spent a couple of years in America, so had plenty of time to learn."

"What were you doing there?"

He picked up his glass and emptied it again.

"Skiing is becoming very popular over there, and they don't have enough instructors, so I went over to teach Americans to ski." He told me about his time in America, and why he decided to come back to France. '*European women are more interesting than American women*' was the basic tenet. I could guess what he really meant by 'interesting'.

The girl I'd come out with interrupted to ask if I was okay if she went off with the guy she'd met. I let her go. I was free to play my favourite sport. Picking up my glass, I emptied it and placed it back on the table. Both were refilled instantly.

"Are you trying to get me drunk?"

He smiled. "Not too drunk."

My turn to smile. "What for?"

"Whatever you want."

"What makes you think I want anything?"

"If you didn't, you wouldn't be flirting."

I opened my mouth to deny the accusation but realised he was right. We were flirting, and I was enjoying it. Clearly, he was as well. I was obviously his target for tonight.

"What did you have in mind?"

"Have you ever had a sauna?"

"No."

"Very healthy and invigorating. Relaxing too."

"Don't tell me, you just happen to know where there's one we can use."

"Of course. Not far away. Very private."

"Private?"

"Sure, just in case you want anything else." He broke into a broad grin.

I laughed. "Not shy, are you?"

"No. Just honest. If you're not interested, I won't mind." He looked me up and down. "Disappointed, maybe."

But I was interested. Well, you can't go on holiday without at least one mindless fuck, can you? Minutes later, he led me out to his car; a VW Beetle, with the obligatory skis strapped to the roof bars. We got in, and off we went, to God knows where.

We were quiet as he drove through the town and turned onto a road leading up the hill towards the treeline. I was quietly excited. The obstler had warmed me right through, and the flirting had also worked its magic. As we left the town behind, the snow was higher on either side of the road, which got steadily narrower. Finally, he turned off the road into a gap between the trees, that was strangely clear of snow.

"Here we are," he said, getting out of the car.

I got out and looked around; he saw my puzzlement.

"Don't worry, it's just down this path." He held out his hand, which I took, and he led the way down a well-trodden track. We only went about twenty yards, before we found ourselves in an open area with a modest log cabin in the centre, and a huge pile of logs seemingly propping it up. I could hear the hum of a small generator somewhere nearby. Walking towards it, he took a key from his pocket and opened the front door.

"Is this your place?" I asked.

"Sometimes."

He was being evasive, but I let it go. There was a dying fire in the grate, and he threw a few logs on, bringing it back to life.

"I will just check the sauna." With that, he disappeared through a door at the end of the room. It didn't really look lived in but was warm and cosy enough. Rugs on the floor, a few chairs and a table. A small but functional kitchen area.

"It will be ready in five minutes," he said, reappearing through the door. "Would you like another drink?"

"More obstler?"

"If you like, but there is also wine or beer here."

"I think wine might be better; I don't want to miss anything."

"Don't worry, I don't want you to, either."

He poured me a glass and opened a beer for himself. Then poked the fire and moved a couple of sheepskin rugs in front of it.

He smiled at me. "Just in case."

"In case of what?"

"In case we have any energy left after the sauna."

"Does a sauna use a lot of energy, then?"

"Depends what you do in it."

"What were you thinking of?"

"The same thing you are."

He was right, and I stopped playing the game. I moved towards the door to the sauna and held out my hand. "Come on then, let's stop thinking and start doing."

"Ah, a girl who likes to lead. Fine by me. But we can't go into the sauna with our clothes on."

"Of course not, that would be so wrong." I stopped and took off my jacket. Sitting down, I took my boots and woollen socks off. I peeled my jumper over my head, the t-shirt followed, and I kicked my trousers off. Leaving me in my bra and knickers. He was still watching me, a faint smile on his face. I stood up straight, folded my arms across my chest, and looked back at him.

"Well?"

He got undressed more quickly than I would have thought possible; everything off before I could take it all in. He was rather dishy; well-built with lots of muscle, but not overdone. And a dick that was ready for action, but not desperate. He tried to copy my stance, folding his arms.

"Well?" He fired back at me.

I shrugged, unhooked my bra, and stepped out of my knickers.

"That is better, I think," he said, and led the way out to the sauna.

It was quite a small room; all wood, with two long benches at different heights along one wall. They were covered with towels. A metal basket in one corner was filled with rocks, with a bowl of water next to it. Some bunches of twigs hung on the wall.

"As this is your first time, just sit and relax."

I did; it was warm, but not as hot as I had expected. I sat on the higher bench, and he sat on the lower one. We were quiet for a couple of minutes, then he got up, and threw a small cup of water on the stones. They hissed and spat, and an unexpected blast of hot steam engulfed me.

"Now, I cleanse you. Lie down."

I laid out flat on my front, and he sat on the lower tier. For the first time, his hand touched my naked body and really went to work. With gentle but firm pressure, he started to massage my body from head to toe. The steam and my sweat were enough to lubricate his hands flowing over my skin, kneading every muscle. It was wonderful, and I allowed my moans and groans to tell him so. A few times, he allowed his hands to drift down between my thighs but didn't linger.

After a few minutes, he asked me to turn over, which I did with relish. He repeated the treatment on my front, and this time, spent some time on my breasts and nipples. Then he worked closer and closer to my sex. I needed it and opened my legs to encourage him. I tensed as his fingers first touched my clit, gently stroking it. Slowly a finger slid into my pussy, then another. And all the while he continued the stroking.

He placed his other hand flat on my groin, and his fingers inside me worked that sensitive sweet spot. Suddenly, I knew I was nearly there; he did too. Without missing a beat, he carried me up and over a full-body orgasm, slowing as I came down. His fingers softly slid out, and he rested his hand on my thigh. I looked up, and he was smiling down at me.

"See, saunas are good for you."

"Yes, good for me. Now. What about you?"

"I like massage too."

"Well, I'm happy to try, but I won't be as good as you are."

"Few are."

He had said it humorously, but I knew a bit about massage, so I got him to lie down on his front and set to work. I wasn't as needy now, so could concentrate on what I was doing. He had a fine body, fit and well-muscled. I worked away, enjoying manipulating his flesh, spending some time on his taut bum. He appeared receptive judging by the little noises coming from him.

I turned him over, and worked on his chest, followed by his legs. His dick was hard now, but I didn't touch it. Moving to his legs, I massaged his toes and feet which he appeared to like.

Coming back up his leg with one hand, I carried on all the way, until I cupped his balls lightly; he flinched briefly. I brought the other hand up to enclose his cock and started to gently stroke and squeeze; the noises got a bit louder.

I pulled his foreskin gently down, continuing until he tensed as it reached full stretch. He looked up at me. I winked, he smiled, and in one movement I bent down and encased his dick with my lips. That brought a first real moan from him; more followed as I made my lips airtight around him and slid gently up and down.

He moved his head to enable him to watch, and I took him as deeply as I could. He dropped his head again, and just lay there enjoying the sensations.

I was being careful; I didn't want him to come yet. I stopped and gently used my hand just to keep him interested. He looked up.

"I'm happy I chose you tonight."

"And you choose a different girl every night ..."

"Not every night." His face widened to a broad grin. "I need a night off every so often."

I gave his cock a sharp tug; he jumped.

"You asked. I told you I was always honest."

"I know; just remember what I've got in my hand."

"How could I forget."

I noticed the twigs on the wall. "What are those for?"

"Ah, part of the ritual. I will show you."

I let him go, and he got up and took one of its hook.

"Stand up."

As I did so, he immediately started striking my body with the bunch; I shrieked as he did so, but he didn't stop. My back, my front, my bum, my tits, my legs. It wasn't hard or particularly painful, but it had surprised me. He was laughing as he played the twigs all over my body; finally stopping and sitting down.

"It's good for you; brings out the toxins."

I held out my hand, "In that case, let me rid you of some toxins."

He happily handed me the bunch and stood up. I then used it on him; all over. I was slightly disappointed, then quite excited that he seemed to love it. I even used them lightly on his dick a few times, but all he did was push his groin forward. I noticed that his dick was rigid now, and I just wanted it. I stopped beating him.

"Sit down." He did so, and without ceremony, I knelt on the bench, legs either side of him, and grabbed his dick. A quick shuffle and I lowered myself onto him, sliding all the way down in one movement. He leaned back slightly and was able to rest his elbows on the bench above. I watched him, as I started to move up and down. I didn't know whether he could or would offer a second round, but I had decided he was going to come this time. I alternated between grinding backwards and forwards, and sliding up and down, knowing that I wasn't far from a second orgasm either. He knew too.

"So, who comes first?" He was smiling again.

"This time we both are."

We forgot everything else; I rode him, he held my hips, almost lifting me up and down, until I heard a groan deep in his throat. He held me down on his dick and rocked me to and fro. I knew I was near; so was he. I felt him spasm and jerk inside me, grunting as he did, and my orgasm came too.

After a few minutes, he took a deep breath.

"I think we've had enough time in here."

I realised I was very hot ... and very sweaty.

"Yes. I'm rather warm." I gently climbed off him and put a hand between my legs.

"Use one of the towels, I always wash them."

I cleaned myself off. Then he suddenly scooped me up in his arms.

"Time to cool off."

He carried me to the door, turned around, and pushed it open with his back. He walked through the hallway to the door into the cabin, but instead of pushing that one, he moved to another door to the side. Again, using his back, he pushed at that one.

A wall of freezing cold air hit me, and I realised – too late – that we were outside. In front of us was three feet of snow. As my brain slowly realised what was about to happen, it did. I found myself flying through the air before landing, naked, in the crisp white drift.

My body went through a variety of reactions; all in one instant. My breathing stopped; my heart missed a beat. I screamed. I heard a loud laugh, and Armand threw himself into the snow beside me and started rolling around. I lay there, still trying to catch my breath, as the cold penetrated my body.

"Roll around; you'll love it."

I cautiously tried it, and as my body got more used to the shock, I had to admit, it did feel good. Strange sensations started to appear. From my bum, my breasts, and between my legs, as areas that had been very hot, got confused as to why they were suddenly so cold. After no more than a minute or so, he stood up and offered me his hand.

"Come. It works well to cool down after the sauna, but too long, and bits will start dropping off."

I took his hand, and he scooped me into his arms again. Going back indoors, he carried me to the rugs in front of the fire and put me down.

"See, they are useful."

I was shivering now but moved closer to the fire, and soon welcomed its warmth.

"Another drink?"

"Got any of that obstler?"

"Of course."

He brought me a glass, which I took in one throw.

"Don't worry, you'll soon warm up."

"If you say so."

"Of course. Then we can carry on."

"Oh?"

"If you want to, of course."

I looked over at him, standing confidently naked in front of the fire.

"Yes. I think that might be good."

It was.

Much later that night, Armand dropped me back at the chalet. As I crept into the room, Pat stirred.

"Is that you, Mary? I was getting a bit worried. Are you all right?"

"Oh, yes thanks."

"Good night, was it?"

"Yes, it was."

"So, who was he?"

"Not telling."

"Spoilsport!"

"Goodnight, Pat."

"Goodnight, Mary."

By the end of the week, we had had a great holiday and only had to endure the long coach journey home. We got bored.

"Would you go skiing again?" Pat asked.

I considered for a while. "Well, it's been fun, but most of the fun happened without skis, so I doubt it. You?"

"Same here. I like to do stuff where I can actually stand up."

"Perhaps we could go somewhere else next time?"

"I'm up for that if you are."

The French countryside rolled by the windows, and we both fell asleep. When we woke up, we were driving into the ferry complex.

"So where were you the night you rolled in at three in the morning?

"Was it really three?

"Yes. That's why I was a bit worried."

"Oh, sorry, Pat. I didn't realise it was that late."

He grinned, "I'll forgive you if you tell all."

"I didn't think you'd be interested. And no, I'm not going into detail."

"Spoilsport. He must have been good."

"Not bad."

"And ..."

"That's all you're getting."

The coach rolled onto the ferry, and we began the final leg of the journey.

"Are you keeping in touch with this mystery man?"

"God, no. It was no one special, just Armand."

He turned slowly to look at me.

"Armand?"

"Yes."

"Our instructor, Armand?"

"Yes."

I wasn't quite sure what his surprise was. Suddenly, he burst out laughing. I was baffled.

"What?" I said. "He's good looking, and, for your information, bloody good."

He looked at me, with a real twinkle in his eyes.

"Oh, I know he is. I had him last night."

Chapter 8 – All Change

Soon after we got back from holiday, Helena asked to see Patrick and me. We immediately wondered what we'd done wrong, but we needn't have worried.

"You may have noticed," she began, after we sat down in her office, "some tension in chambers recently." She wasn't wrong; the clerk's office had continued as always. But we had heard a few arguments between the partners, and even Henry had made a few comments under his breath about one or two members of the office.

"Well," she continued, "my colleagues and I have been having some discussions about the setup and future direction of this partnership. Unfortunately, we can't agree, so we've decided to split up." Pat and I looked at one another. "Eight partners are staying, and three of us are leaving." She paused, studying us. "Edward, Harriet and I intend to establish our own chambers and build it the way we want it. We'd like you two to come with us." We glanced at one another again. "Patrick, you'd be senior clerk, because of your experience."

I could see that Pat was thinking as quickly as he could. "But what would happen here? Henry would be left on his own. How would they cope?"

Helena sighed. "Frankly, Patrick, I'm not bothered. In the discussions, we were given permission to take you both with us if you want to come. It's fine if you don't; your jobs here will still be safe. But if we are going to build a new chambers from scratch, we need to hit the ground running, and you two can both do that. We can talk about salaries and commissions, but they'll be no less than here."

I'd had a bit of time to think. "Where will you be based, Helena?"

She shrugged. "No idea, Mary. We're still working on finding offices, but it won't be too far."

"When do you need an answer?" Pat asked.

"I know it's short notice, but as soon as possible, please. If one or both of you come with us, it'll be one less headache for us."

As we left Helena's office, Pat turned to me. "Let's go and grab a coffee or something. We need to think."

We spent an hour or so in a café around the corner, going over the news. It had come as a surprise, but the more we thought about it, the more attractive the move became. It should be a much lighter environment. It was a promotion for Patrick, an informal promotion for me.

"But poor old Henry would be left on his own." Pat had a soft spot for the old grouch. "He couldn't cope with all our work."

"Well, I guess they'll have to get someone new in."

"But why let both of us go at the same time?"

"Perhaps our faces don't fit. Let's be honest, mine never has with some of the partners."

"I suppose so."

We each thought about it overnight. Next morning, we went together to see Helena and told her we wanted to move. She seemed delighted and relieved. Back in our office, Henry looked up from his desk.

"I suppose you two are deserting me?"

We mumbled replies, rather embarrassed. Amazingly, Henry smiled.

"Don't worry. We all have to leave the nest some time."

The next few weeks were a blur. New offices were found, not far away. An experienced clerk was brought in to help Henry, and replace us, and we were the first to move into the new chambers. Pat and I worked fifteen-hour days.

Equipping the offices, arranging the thousand and one things that we didn't even know we needed until we didn't have them. After a few weeks of this mayhem, things settled down, and we got into a new routine. A routine that Pat and I created. In time, it proved to work very well.

***

Catherine called me one day; out of the blue. Since she had married, we hadn't seen each other regularly. We met at family events, and Christmas and birthdays. I'd visit occasionally, to see the girls; Sally and Charlotte. Wonderful girls. Sally was the more serious; Charlie was more outgoing. Catherine loved them, but she took a strict line with them. Tony seemed to be away most of the time.

"Mary, I'm worried about Mum."

"Oh. Why's that?"

"She said something to me yesterday that I can't stop thinking about."

"Which was?"

"Something about not being here much longer. I asked what she meant, but she wouldn't talk about it. Can … can you try?"

"Sure. I'll drop in tonight."

I thought Catherine was probably worrying unduly. But she turned out to be right. Mum had a couple of lumps in her breast. Had had them for months. But she didn't tell anyone and was too scared to get them checked out. By the time we insisted, it was too late. Then she followed Dad by refusing any treatment. She died five months after Catherine first called me.

It briefly brought Catherine and me closer together. Dealing with Mum's illness; her death and the aftermath. We had a few open chats about Mum and Dad, growing up, the paths we had chosen. I noticed a sadness in her, which didn't really surprise me. I asked if she was happy, and she brushed it off, unconvincingly. To give him his due, Tony stayed around while we sorted everything out, and helped a lot.

But when everything was done, he went back to his disappearing act. I saw a lot of the girls for a few months as well. They were happy with Catherine, but there was a distance between them and Tony. By all accounts, they didn't see him very much.

When it was all over, we did see a bit more of each other. I think Catherine was lonely. She didn't seem to have many friends, and with Mum gone, she was more comfortable with me. And the girls now had no grandparents, so Auntie Mary was their only close relative. I enjoyed seeing them, but Catherine was still wary of my influence. That would never change.

***

Pat's life changed too. He met Craig. They met in one of the gay bars and hit it off instantly. Within a couple of months, Craig moved in with Pat. I liked him. He was smart, funny, and handsome. He never seemed quite sure of me but was always polite and friendly. One morning, I noticed that Pat was a bit weary.

"You all right, Pat?"

"Yea. It's just Craig."

"Oh, sorry." I was afraid I'd strayed into private strife. "Problems?"

He looked at me. "Oh no … He's just … insatiable."

I burst out laughing. "Well, if that's your only problem, I've got no sympathy whatsoever."

Now it was his turn to laugh. "Yea. I guess things could be worse."

"I wish I had the same problem."

"Ooh, losing your touch, Mary?"

"Honestly Pat, I don't know. But it sounds like I'm definitely not getting as much as you."

And I wasn't. Admittedly since our holiday, we'd been rushed off our feet working. But I'd still been out and about and not come across anyone that I'd even fancied one night with. Most guys around my age were now married, and not yet old enough to be divorced. Those that weren't; well, you could generally see why. I also realised that I didn't really have a circle of friends anymore. Again, they were married, having kids. Too busy to go out much. Even Pat was now paired off. For the first time in my life, I felt a bit lonely.

Chapter 9 – The Student

I joined a social club. Deciding I wanted to just meet new people, rather than just look for lovers, I found a local group that seemed to organise all sorts of things. From meals in local pubs to holidays abroad. I decided to dip my toe in and went to a couple of meetups. They were a mixed bunch, all types, all ages. But they all seemed friendly enough. Nobody tried too hard; the purpose wasn't to impress but to have fun.

Over the course of a few months, I joined theatre trips, country walks, museum visits. Even an outward-bound weekend, abseiling and rock-climbing. I soon noticed a few other members who appeared to go on most of the events I did, and we got to know one another. I made some good friends; one or two, I'm still in touch with after all these years.

And I noticed Paul. If I went on a trip to a museum or a gallery, he was always there. He seemed engrossed. He was also a bit apart. He talked to us, but never initiated conversation. After seeing him a few times, I looked more closely. He was older than me; perhaps late thirties. Tall, slim, not handsome, but perfectly acceptable. Although he attended many events, he always seemed quite happy on his own.

One weekend, I joined a trip to London. A meal was booked for Friday evening, and on Saturday we were going to see Evita. But the rest of the time was our own. Some like-minded people paired up to visit attractions, others went off on their own.

I determined to go to the National Gallery, and just wander. I hadn't been for a few years. When I arrived, I had to decide where to go. The place was far too big to take everything in at one visit. After checking the floorplan, I chose three galleries almost at random and set off.

Art has a strange effect on people. Wandering through a gallery with thirty paintings, you'll walk straight past some, pause at others. Then you will find a painting that makes you stand and stare. Oblivious to everyone else. You probably won't be able to explain why. But that's all right; just stand, and take it in.

Partway through the second gallery, I spotted Paul. He was sitting on one of the benches, just staring at a painting in front of him. I worked my way around the room to see what he was looking at. I couldn't make much of it at first. A rather abstract image; lots going on, but none of it immediately obvious.

"Hi, Paul."

He gave a slight start as he came out of his reverie and looked up at me.

"Oh, hello, Mary."

"Did I disturb you?"

"Yes ... I mean ... no. Sorry, what I mean is ... I was rather lost in ..." His voice trailed off.

"In that one?"

"Yes."

I motioned at the bench. "May I?"

"Uh, yes. Of course."

I sat down beside him and noticed he shifted slightly away from me.

"What's it called?"

"Well, the label's not very helpful, I'm afraid. It just says 'allegorical painting' by an unknown artist. Probably French, probably nineteenth century."

"So, a bit of a mystery, then."

"Yes."

"But it called you?"

"Yes."

"Funny isn't it how a particular work will suddenly sing out to you."

He smiled briefly. "It's not just me, then?"

"No. I wish it happened to everyone. I see so many people racing through the galleries, glancing briefly at the more famous stuff. Most of them don't stop at all before hitting the café or the gift shop."

"I know. I could sit here and look at almost every painting for hours."

"Well, I'd be a bit more selective, but I know what you mean."

He smiled. "Perhaps I exaggerated a little."

We sat quietly for a while, contemplating the picture.

"Well," I finally said. "It may be an allegory, but I have no idea what of."

"Honestly, neither have I. I've been looking at it for half an hour, and I'm more uncertain now than when I started. I just like it."

"There is a lot going on, it's beautifully drawn and it captivated you. Perhaps that's enough?"

"That sounds a bit childish, doesn't it?"

I looked at him. "Not at all. We can't always explain why we're attracted to things, can we?"

"Perhaps it's a gift from God." The response surprised me, and I thought I heard more than a little sarcasm in his voice.

"I don't know about that, Paul. I'm afraid God and I are not close."

He turned to me. "No?"

"Nope."

"You don't believe?"

"No."

He turned away slowly. I had an uneasy feeling that I was about to get an earnest exhortation to turn to Jesus or an invitation to a prayer meeting. But no; just three words.

"I envy you."

I turned towards him in surprise. For the first time, I noticed a sadness in his expression; a weariness. I wasn't sure how to respond. I think he sensed my discomfort.

"Sorry. I normally avoid discussing religion, but it's hard in a place stuffed full of so many religious works."

"Oh, it's not a problem. I just wasn't sure if you were about to launch into an attempt to convert me."

He gave a mirthless laugh. "No. That's one thing I'd never do. Not now."

It was all getting a bit heavy, so I suggested as it was lunchtime, we went and got something to eat in one of the cafes or restaurants. After a little hesitation, he agreed. I was intrigued. He was clearly intelligent, but there was something about him that seemed to weigh him down. He was diffident, and as I'd noticed before, tended to avoid company. So, was he coming to lunch simply to avoid being rude?

We found a restaurant at the end of the next gallery and didn't have to wait long for a table. The menu was short but fine, and we soon ordered.

"What do you do, Mary?"

"Barrister's clerk."

He looked up sharply. "Really? I didn't know women did that."

"Well, you do now."

"Sorry … didn't mean to …"

"Relax, Paul. I'm joking. I know I'm a rare species. But I love it. What about you?"

"Accountant. And I hate it. Hate pretty much everything in my life actually." This was said with some feeling.

"Why not do something else?"

He was playing with a glass in his hand. "Do you know that Monty Python sketch? The one where the man goes to the employment adviser?"

I knew it. "The accountant who wants to be a lion tamer?"

"The very same. Mr Anchovy. It could have been written about me. I want to change, but I guess … I guess I haven't got the courage. I'm stuck in a rut."

"So why not make a plan? Decide what you want to do, and work towards it. Perhaps skip the lions, though."

"Not practical, really. See, I'm married."

I was even more intrigued now. "Your wife isn't in the group, is she?"

"Oh no. We lead largely separate lives."

"Not happy?"

"I'm discovering just how unhappy it's possible to be."

"Why not get divorced?"

Another of his mirthless laughs. He sighed. I think he weighed up whether to continue. "We've been married for twelve years. We're both from very religious families, and divorce would be unthinkable. At least, to her and both our families."

"But not you?"

He was still toying with his glass.

"I've struggled with my faith for a while now. How can God want someone to be unhappy all their lives? But I can't let go completely."

The earlier comment now made sense.

"Any children?" I asked, immediately regretting it, as he looked hard at me.

"I believe you need to share a bed to make that happen."

"Ah …"

He slumped into his chair. "I'm sorry, Mary. I didn't mean to shock you."

I laughed; he looked puzzled.

"Paul, I doubt you could shock me. Although I'm not sure about the other way around." He reddened slightly. "I do what I want, when I want, with whoever I want. I'm sure your wife would have some words to describe me; not necessarily complimentary."

"Nothing she ever says is complimentary."

The food finally arrived, and we started eating.

"Was your marriage never happy?"

He paused, thinking.

"We've got nothing in common, except originally our faith. We never became friends. Never got to know one another."

"But you must have been lovers once?"

He looked at me, clearly shocked by my candid question.

"Sorry, Paul. I guess we move in different circles. I didn't mean to be rude. Ignore me."

We ate a little more. After a while, he restarted, somewhat hesitantly.

"You and your friends talk about your … private lives?"

"Sex lives, you mean?" He looked down at his food. "Sometimes. I'm pretty open with my closest friends."

"Are you married?"

"God, no. I've been having too much fun."

"And marriage can't be fun?"

"You tell me."

The mirthless laugh again. "Point taken. When Esther and I got married, we were both virgins. We were twenty-seven. I guess that seems pretty weird to you?"

"I wouldn't judge, Paul. We're all different. What's right for me, isn't right for others."

"Do you know what happened?"

"Are you sure you want to tell me?"

"Yes, I do. I want to tell someone. We had sex twice on our honeymoon."

I looked at him, wondering where this was going. A café in the National Gallery was a hell of a place for an intimate confession.

"And that's it. Esther hated it. She was horrified. I'm not sure she knew much about it, really. God knows, I knew little enough. She's never come near me again."

I must have allowed my surprise to show.

"It's true. Can you imagine that?"

"Honestly? No, I couldn't. I've led a fairly ... active love life. I wouldn't accept that situation for twelve weeks, let alone twelve years."

"Do I seem bitter to you?"

"No. Not bitter. A little melancholy, perhaps. There's a sadness in your eyes sometimes."

He smiled a rare smile. "Are you surprised?"

"Not now. But how does your wife agree to you coming on these events?"

His smile became a broad grin.

"Ah, that's where her own faith lets her down. She believes so strongly in our marriage vows that she cannot imagine either of us breaking them. She lets me do my own thing. I think she quite likes me out of the house. Mind you, I haven't broken them, so perhaps she's right."

"But haven't you been tempted?"

"Tempted; yes. But look at me. I'm thirty-nine. I'm a boring accountant. I've been married for twelve years, with no prospect of divorce and my experience of romance and sex are, well, minimal, shall we say. Who'd be interested?"

I was about to make a flirty comment, but he continued.

"And even if I came across someone, I'd be scared stiff. To be so naïve at my age, it would only end in disaster."

I went to reply, but again, he went on.

"And honestly, Mary? I'm too much of a coward. I can't imagine approaching a woman. I never did it when I was young; how could I do it now?"

He had run out of steam at last. He just sat there, poking the remaining food on his plate with his fork.

"Perhaps you need a woman who makes the first move."

"Why would they?" He thought for a moment. "Do women do that?"

I stifled a laugh. "Yes, Paul. All the time. I've done it all my life."

He studied me for a few seconds, before looking away.

"But," I continued, "would that be too much for you? Not your sort of woman?"

He looked embarrassed. "I don't know Mary. It's never happened to me. And I've no idea what my sort of woman is."

We finished lunch, and I asked if he wanted to wander around another gallery or two. Hesitantly, he agreed, and I let him choose. We spent a couple of hours amiably debating several works. I soon realised that he knew a lot more about art than me. Not in a pretentious way, but I learnt quite a lot. I was enjoying Paul's company.

We were due to see Evita that evening, after going out for a pre-Theatre meal, so we grabbed a cream tea mid-afternoon.

"Have you studied art, Paul?"

"No, but it's always been an interest of mine. A passion, almost. I used to draw and paint when I was younger, but my family weren't keen – painted images, and all that – and Esther always mocked my efforts. So, I gave up. But I've always read about it and come to galleries and exhibitions when I can."

"I guess this group is a godsend for you."

"It's been something of a lifesaver, to be honest. I joined three years ago. Esther assumes that we're a bunch of boring no-hopers, and I do nothing to disabuse her. In truth, although I don't mix that much, everyone is always friendly and welcoming. Without it, I think I'd go mad."

"No social circle at home?"

"Not really. Oh, my colleagues are all right, but they know Esther, so nothing is private. Then the people we both know are all like her. A social event with them is like going to a funeral."

I laughed; he joined in. We walked slowly back to the hotel. He asked me about my life; I told him a somewhat edited version. I thought it best not to frighten him too much. I was forming a plan.

The evening passed easily. The whole group went out for a quick meal, and then on to the theatre. There were about twenty-five of us, and I reflected on what Paul had said. It was a friendly, welcoming environment. I noticed him occasionally chatting to people and wondered how different he was at home. I guessed he wasn't what you'd call henpecked, but he probably took the path of least resistance. Just for an easy life. Did I feel sorry for him? Perhaps a little.

But I was also drawn to him for another reason. He hadn't flirted; he hadn't tried to chat me up. It hadn't even crossed his mind. Whether that was his lack of experience, or that he was resigned to his life, I wasn't sure. But it had meant that we talked simply as two people, with no under-current. That had been refreshing; and curiously attractive.

When we left the theatre, a few people went off to find bars, clubs and anything else London had to offer on a Saturday night. I watched Paul. I guessed he would join the small group heading back to the hotel, and when he did, I tagged along. Most of them headed up to their rooms; Paul included.

"Off to bed already, Paul?"

"Oh, well. I'm not one for sitting and drinking."

"At least keep me company for a nightcap."

It was a budget hotel, so the lobby doubled as the lounge and the breakfast area. We headed towards the small bar in one corner.

"What are you having, Paul?"

"I'll get them."

"A girl can't buy you a drink?"

He looked a bit chastened and smiled.

"OK, Mary. I'll have a whiskey, please."

I got the drinks, and we settled into a couple of chairs.

"Did you enjoy Evita?" I asked.

"Wasn't it wonderful? I love musicals; well, all theatre really. I'd never seen one until a couple of years ago."

"Was that with the group?"

"Yes."

"What was the first one you saw?"

He paused; looked at me with a slight grin. "Hair."

I laughed. "I bet you didn't know where to look."

"Oh, I knew where to look all right. But I'd never seen anything like it."

"Come on, there's more nudity on TV."

"We don't have a TV," he said flatly.

I looked at him. "You're kidding?"

"No. Esther thinks it's immoral."

"God. She's not related to Mary Whitehouse, is she?"

"No. But she thinks she's doing a good job."

He went quiet and sipped his drink. The area was nearly empty now. Most people were either still out partying or had gone to bed.

"I thought you'd have gone on somewhere with the others, Mary."

"No, not tonight. I've got other plans."

"Oh, right. Anything nice?"

I leaned towards his ear. "You get four more whiskies from the bar, bring them to room 358 in ten minutes, and I'll show you."

He looked at me blankly. Slowly, understanding began to dawn.

"Why ...? Are you ...?"

"Making the first move? Yes. Interested?"

I think he was genuinely lost for words. He twisted in his seat.

"I don't know what to say."

"Are you interested?"

"Yes," he answered in a whisper. "But ... well ..."

"But you're nervous," I said, smiling.

He almost squeaked a reply. "Nervous? I'm terrified."

I leaned towards him, again. "Well, Mr accountant. I'll be a very gentle lioness for you to tame. No claws. Just a kitten, really. See you in ten minutes. 358."

I gave him a kiss on the cheek, got up, and headed to the lift. I had no idea if he would come to my room or not. At that moment, I don't think he did either.

He came. I'd gone back to my room and freshened up. I hadn't brought any glamorous underwear, so decided to take everything off, and just put a lightweight dressing gown on. Ten minutes; nothing. Eleven, twelve. I began to think he'd cried off.

But after fifteen minutes, there was a faint knock on my door. I opened it to find Paul standing a little awkwardly in front of me, holding a tray with four glasses. I saw him do a comedy double-take when he noticed I was wearing a robe.

"Hi, Paul. Come in."

"Uh, thanks."

I shut the door after him.

"I thought you weren't coming."

He looked in my direction without looking me in the eye.

"Well, Mary. You took me by surprise. I had to think. So, I had another drink."

"And ...?"

He took a deep breath. "Well, I'm here."

I walked up to him, and gently kissed him. "Good. Now put that tray down somewhere, otherwise, I might mistake you for a waiter."

He was very nervous. To use his word, I think he was terrified. He put the tray on the dressing table and turned around. But he didn't know what to do with himself.

"Paul?"

"Mmm."

"Sit down on the bed."

When he did, looking down at the floor, I sat by his side.

"Just relax, Paul."

"I … I don't really know what I'm doing."

"I know exactly what I'm doing." He smiled. "So, leave it to me. I'll lead, you follow. Deal?"

He finally looked me in the eye. "Why are you doing this?"

"Because I want to. Because you're a nice guy. Because I love sex. Because I fancy sex with a nice guy."

"Not because you feel sorry for me."

"No, Paul. Although the idea of taking an innocent man and moulding him to my wicked needs has its attractions."

I could tell from his reaction that he didn't really understand what I meant. He would.

"So, do we have a deal?"

He took another deep breath. "Yes."

Looking back, the rest of the night was rather special. The situation was unusual for me. I was used to men who knew what they were doing. At least, they knew what they wanted, even if they didn't always worry about what I wanted. Paul knew virtually nothing about sex, apart from the basic mechanics. He knew nothing about the infinite variety. Little about his own body, and nothing about the female body. I set out to begin his education.

"Good. There's no hurry. We've got all night."

He looked at me in surprise. "All night?"

"Yes. Unless you're planning on going anywhere."

"No. But … what …? I can't …"

I guessed what he was thinking.

"Sex with Esther was short, am I right? She just lay there."

He looked down again. "Yes."

"And you were the only one who came."

He looked at me, puzzlement on his face. "Well, yes. That's how it is, isn't it?"

"No. That's not how it should be. You do know women orgasm too, don't you?"

I could see his mind racing. At that moment, he did look like a little boy lost. Quietly, he replied. "I've heard about it, but I wasn't sure if it was true. How do I ...? What ...?"

I put a finger to his lips.

"Shush. Don't overthink it. This isn't a theory class. We're going for the practical, so let's just see what happens."

I stood up and gently got him to his feet. Giving him a kiss, I started to undress him, as he stood rooted to the spot. His face was a mixture of excitement and terror. I knew I had to take some of the tension away. He was down to his underpants now. I looked down; a nice bulge sticking out. I stood in front of him and put my arms over his shoulders.

"You're tense, right?"

"I guess it's obvious, uh?"

"Just a bit. So, what I'm going to do is lay you down on the bed and give you a bit of a massage to relax you. Ever had a massage?"

"No."

"I thought not." I moved a couple of paces back, and swiftly undid my robe, and dropped it to the floor. I watched his face as he let his eyes wander over my naked body. I gave him the chance to have a good look. After a while, he let out a little groan.

"You'll have to lose those, Paul." I pointed to his pants. I saw a faint look of panic in his eyes. Then he gave a gentle shrug, pushed them down, and lifted them off his foot. His dick looked inviting; quite thick.

"We're just two naked people among thousands, planning to have some fun. Now lay on the bed, face down."

He took the opportunity to escape my gaze and laid on the bed. I only had some baby oil to use, but it would have to do. He tensed as I gently straddled his thighs. Leaning forward, I kissed his neck and moved to his ear.

"Try to relax, Paul. Think of the now. Not the past; not the future. Just concentrate on your senses."

A mumbled reply told me he had at least heard me. I sat back up and poured a little oil on his back, and then onto my hands. Starting between his shoulder blades, I slid my hands over his body. I wasn't intending to give him a full massage; just enough to relax him, and help him forget his feelings of ... what?

Fear?

Guilt?

I could only guess.

As my hands roamed over his torso, I wondered what it was like to feel so badly about sex. I never had, so struggled to understand. I had already seen that Paul had a fine body; not sculpted, not muscular. But defined, not an ounce of fat. Looking down, I noticed that he had a nice tight bum too; not bad for a guy of nearly forty. And I moved my hands to those buttocks now. Slowly kneading them. I moved back slightly so that I could reach the backs of his thighs. As I moved my hands over his skin, I let them slip lower between his legs. I noticed his thighs move closer.

"Ah, ah. Let them open."

He relaxed a little, and there was just room to allow a couple of fingers to reach the bedclothes. I moved down, and massaged his legs, spending longer on his feet, as that started to elicit louder groans from him. I had noticed some little noises as I had gone about my work. Whether he was holding back, I wasn't sure. I slowly slid myself all the way back up his body. Deliberately sliding my pussy up one leg. I was surprised by how turned on I was. Returning to his ear, I clamped myself to him.

"How was that?"

"Wonderful." He had said it with a feeling that surprised me.

"A bit more relaxed?"

"Mmm."

"Good. Turn over."

He hesitated for a moment and then flipped over onto his back. His dick was well and truly hard now and stood erect. He tried to tuck it between his legs.

"Leave it, Paul. Be proud of it. It seems to like me."

He grinned, and for the first time, allowed himself to take a good look at my body. I was kneeling by him. He reached out a hand, and touched my side, running his hand around to my back, and then returning to my tummy. I bent down and kissed him.

"How does it feel."

He thought for a moment. "Smooth ... soft ... warm. Wonderful."

Sitting up, I poured some more oil onto his tummy, and using one hand, slid my hand over his abdomen and chest. Slowly going lower until on each circle, I was running over the top of his pubic hair. He tensed each time I did so. I took some more oil and moved down to attend to his legs and feet. He finally seemed to have relaxed, although he was still watching me. Taking in my body.

I moved my hands up his legs, but this time, I carried on, running my fingers all the way over his balls. He moaned. I continued over his dick, pushing it down onto his belly; letting it spring back, as I went past the end. He flinched.

I lay down beside him. Kissing him, I brought my hand back to his dick. Slowly running my fingers along it, wrapping them around it. Starting to stroke it. He was making little noises, but I realised he was holding back.

"Let yourself go, Paul. Make all the noise you want."

He immediately got louder, as I caressed his dick and balls. He opened his legs slightly, and I could get my fingers down below his sac. This brought a crescendo of moans. I had him now. He'd stopped holding back. I let my other hand slide down between my own legs. I was wet; time to relax us both. I leant close to his ear.

"Now I'm going to show you what sex is really like, Paul. Do you want to use a condom?"

He looked at me. "We have to, don't we?"

"I'm on the pill."

"Oh. OK. But I don't want to hurt you."

I took his hand and placed it between my legs. He felt the wetness and looked puzzled.

"You see, Paul. See what you can do to a woman?"

I sat up. He was watching closely. I lifted my leg and straddled him. I might have played with him for a while; running my pussy up and down his dick. But I decided that could wait. So, I shuffled my hips, and held his dick, as I placed my pussy on its head. Looking down at him, I slowly lowered myself. Easing onto him, smoothly but firmly. I had been right, he was thick, and I grunted as I finally rested on him; my pussy full. I leaned down over him.

"Does that feel good?"

"Unbelievable."

"Believe it. You ain't seen nothing yet."

I sat back up, and placing my hands on his hips, I started to rock backwards and forwards. I knew I wanted that first orgasm, and I didn't know whether he would last long. So, I worked on myself, rocking, and using one hand to play with myself. He was watching me closely. I soon felt myself building and ground harder. Then, it happened. I spasmed on his dick a few times, a grunt accompanying each one. He was lying almost motionless. As I finally leaned down over him, I found out why.

"Are you OK? Did I hurt you?"

I giggled as my breathing returned to normal. "No Paul, I'm fine. You've just seen a girl have an orgasm on your dick."

He looked a bit confused briefly, then smiled. "Oh. Is that what happens? I ... I didn't know."

I moved to his ear.

"I've had my first orgasm." I lifted my hips and lowered them again. "Now for yours." I started to slide up and down his dick more firmly. "Does that feel good?"

"Mmm."

"Just let it happen, Paul."

I sat up, still rising and falling. I put one hand behind me and started to squeeze his balls. That did it. He cried out, grabbed the bedclothes, and stared up at me. I felt his dick jerk inside me, and his hips twitched as he came. I slowed down, let go of his balls, and leaned down onto him. He put his arms around me; still breathing heavily.

After a pause, I pulled up a little so I could see his face. He had been silently crying.

"Are you all right?"

"Yes," he said. "Sorry. That was ... well, I can't find the words. Just a bit ... emotional. Thank you."

"No need for thanks; we both enjoyed round one."

"Round one?"

"Well, we do have all night."

A sheepish grin appeared on his face. "I've got a lot to learn, haven't I?"

"Honestly, Paul? I think you have. And I'm looking forward to teaching you."

After we both cleaned up, we lay on the bed with a whisky each. He kept glancing at my body.

"Don't be shy, Paul. Look as much as you want. I'm happy with my body, and I'm going to teach you all about it. So, you're going to see every bit in minute detail."

"Sorry." He paused. I knew he was wondering whether to tell me something. "Do you know, I've never seen a naked woman this close."

"But ... Esther?"

"We had sex twice, remember? Both times, under the covers with the lights out. It was all over in five minutes. And we've had separate rooms ever since the honeymoon. I've never seen my own wife naked."

I took a risk. "What's she like?"

He thought for a moment. "Quite pretty, actually. When it was first suggested we get married, I was happy enough. At the time, we shared a strong faith, and she was attractive. When I did think about sex, I was very content with how she looked. Even now, she's got a good figure. Fat lot of good it's done me. She's totally uptight about anything to do with sex."

"You mean you're not even sure if she's seen *herself* naked?"

This time, his laugh was easy and natural. "Something like that."

We lay, contentedly for several minutes. This time, he made no secret of exploring my body with his eyes. I made sure my body was placed to give him a good view.

"Mary ..."

"Mmm."

"Well, I understand how a man has an orgasm ... I think."

"Mmm."

"Well, it's sort of ... friction. The stroking."

"There are one or two other ways."

"Oh. OK. But how does a woman have one? Is it the same?"

Well, where to start?

"I don't think I can easily answer that, Paul. Sometimes, it's easy; sometimes, it's hard. And every woman is different."

"So, what do I – "

"Slow down, Paul. I need you to answer a question."

"What's that?"

"Is this a one-off? Or do we have a thing here?"

He thought for quite some time.

"I'll be honest with you, Mary. I'm not divorcing Esther, even though I'd like to. Not yet, anyway."

"That's fine by me, Paul. I like being a free woman. I'm not trying to steal you from her. I'm not looking to get hitched; to you, or anyone else. No commitments; just a lot of fun."

"In that case, yes. If you're interested."

I kissed him. "I am, as it happens. So, in answer to your question; why don't I show you?"

I laid on my front.

"Just explore my body; don't be shy." He wasn't. I lay there, as his hand began to run all over me. Neither of us was needy anymore. He took his time following my curves, caressing every inch. He was being very gentle, and I was enjoying it.

After ten minutes or so, I turned over. He was a little hesitant at first, but got bolder, and was soon toying with my nipples with his fingers. My nipples were always sensitive, as he soon discovered. Eventually, he worked his way down my abdomen but kept circling above it.

"Go on," I prompted him, quietly. He did. His hands went down my thighs and ran up either side of my pussy. He did this for a while, eventually allowing his hand to run over it. After several passes, he let a finger push further between my lips, and slip in.

"Is this OK?"

"Mmm. You carry on. I'll guide you if I need to."

He kept going. He didn't know what he was doing, but that was part of the fun. I steered his fingers in the right direction once or twice. He clearly didn't know his female anatomy but seemed to pick it up quickly. A little heavy-handed, but, in truth, no worse than some more experienced men I'd slept with. I knew he was going to make me come, and as I started to breathe more heavily, he did too. He made the age-old mistake of speeding up.

"Slow down; just carry on doing what you were doing."

And I came. Not a massive orgasm, but who cares? I saw him as I came down, watching me, a faint smile on his face. But also, a look of curiosity. He sat there, while I recovered.

"How many times can a woman have an orgasm?" He asked.

"How long is a piece of string? We all differ. But for me, sometimes once is fine. Sometimes two, three, four, five times? Depends how I feel, and who I'm with."

"Not with a novice, eh?"

"Oh, not necessarily. We'll see, won't we? But how many times can you come?"

He looked at me questioningly. "I don't know. I've never come more than once when I ..."

"Masturbate?"

"Yes."

"Don't be shy, Paul. Everyone does it. It's good for you."

"Do women ...?"

"God. Yes, Paul. We sure do."

"I doubt all do." This was said with a wry grin. I guess the name 'Esther' floated through both our heads.

"Well, perhaps not. But most do. Believe me. Now, shall we find out about you?"

I pushed him onto his back and knelt beside him. Gently lifting his dick, I began to stroke it. It soon responded. Bending down, I started to kiss his balls, gently nibbling his sac, and running my nails over it. His dick was hard now, and I ran my tongue up and down it. I looked up at him to see him staring down. I wondered if he even knew about oral sex; probably not.

Our eyes met, and holding his gaze, I slipped my lips over the head of his dick. His eyes widened, and with a groan, he let his head drop back onto the pillow. I started to slide my lips up and down his shaft, still playing with his balls. He was moaning now; his abdominal muscles tightening and relaxing as I teased him.

I let my fingers drop to stroke that sensitive area between his sac and bum. His hips bucked up off the bed; that was something to work on. His moans suddenly increased; he was close to coming already. I came off his dick and turned my head so that I could lick the bottom of his glans with my tongue.

When I did, he let out a long, low groan, and his breathing increased. Holding his dick in a tight grip, with the skin pulled down hard, I flicked my tongue rapidly from side to side. Suddenly, he tensed, grunted, and came. His dick went into spasm, and his cum shot into the air. After several spurts, I stopped, gently stroking him, while his orgasm subsided.

After a minute or two, he looked down at me.

"Wow. I guess that's a blowjob?"

"Yup. Any good?"

A wicked grin crossed his face. "I'm not sure. I may need to try it again before deciding."

"You're learning fast."

"Oh, Mary. That was fantastic. Do men ... I mean ... on a woman ..."

"Yes, men go down on women too. Not all, though. You don't have to."

"Do you like it?"

"Oh yes. Love it."

"Then I want to do it."

"You're going to make a good student, I think."

We rested again, and at one point, Paul suddenly chuckled. I asked him what was so funny.

"Do you realise something? I've been married for twelve years. You and I have had as much sex in two hours as my wife and I in our whole marriage."

I didn't know quite how to reply; it was a sad thought. There didn't seem to be anything appropriate to say. He sensed my quandary.

"Oh, don't worry. I wasn't being bitter; it just struck me as funny. I feel so good."

"Let's see if we can double the score by the time we leave tomorrow."

We did. And that began a long and fruitful relationship. We only met up on group trips, but we made sure we went on most of them. He was a willing learner; and quick too. Once over his initial nervousness, he wanted to try everything and became a considerate, intelligent lover. We made each other happy.

Our occasional weekends were great for both of us. No baggage; no expectation. We had affection for each other, but never got emotionally entangled.

His confidence gradually returned. I'm not claiming credit, but he started to re-think his life. He started painting and drawing again; despite his wife's derision. He was good; very good. He even had an exhibition at a local gallery, where he sold a few works. Not for vast sums of money, but enough to boost his confidence again.

About three years after we first got involved, he unusually invited me to go away for the weekend. I accepted. We arrived on Friday evening, and I sensed he was a bit distant. After dinner, I eventually found out why.

"Mary," he said when the table was clear. "I've got something I need to tell you."

"OK."

"I'm not sure how to say it. I rehearsed it, but it all seems wrong."

I knew something big was coming but didn't want it to get too heavy. "Well, as long as you don't ask me to marry you or something, just start at the beginning."

"No. No, it's not that. In fact …" he paused. "It's sort of the opposite. I'm divorcing Esther."

He picked up his glass and took a couple of swigs. I played with my glass and watched him. I didn't say anything.

"I'm quitting my job."

He paused again. I think he was willing me to say something. Anything.

"And … I'm moving."

He looked at me pleadingly, waiting for my reply. I stayed silent, and he was forced to continue.

"Which means – "

"Which means that we won't be seeing each other anymore."

"I need to explain – "

I held up my hand. "No, Paul, you don't. No commitments, no expectations. Remember?"

"Yes, but I want to. Please?"

"Go on."

"I've been planning it for a while. I'm buying a house in St Ives. It's only a small cottage, but it'll be fine. And I'm going to paint. I can always find temporary accountancy work if I need it. But I'm doing what I want."

"Good for you."

"I'm sorry I couldn't tell you, but I didn't tell anyone. Not until it was all sorted."

"That's fine, Paul. I'm quite proud of you."

"I couldn't have done it without you, though."

"Rubbish."

"No, Mary. The truth. You've given me the confidence to take my life back. Back from my wife; back from my job." He paused. "And back from ... well, religious control. Thank you."

I smiled. "It was there all along, Paul. Perhaps I just helped you find it."

"Perhaps. Anyway, now you know. And if you want to go home after dinner, I'll understand."

"Do you want to?"

Now confident of himself, he looked down at my body with a grin. "No."

"Good. Neither do I. If this is our last time together, then we're going to spend the weekend enjoying one another."

And we did. It was the last time we were intimate. We did meet up briefly to say goodbye, and it was a bit emotional for both of us. We kept in touch. He loved his new life, and years later, married a sculptor fifteen years younger than him. I hope he still remembered what I taught him. If he did, I think she'd be satisfied with him!

Chapter 10 – Darkness

While I'd been involved with Paul, I'd been happy. We had a great relationship. Yes, it had been part-time, but that suited me. Work had been going well, too. The new chambers had gone from strength to strength. Several new barristers had joined us, and we took on another clerk, Nigel. Which proved to be a good move; for all the wrong reasons.

Pat and Craig were still together, and as happy as ever. They still went out with their old friends, and I occasionally went with them. But this was the eighties. AIDS had appeared. And wreaked havoc; initially within the gay community. And no-one was safe. Several members of the original group I had got to know had died in a short space of time.

Most of the group were much more selective now. And careful. Ignorance was everywhere; it was seen as a 'gay plague', and homophobia grew. There were all sorts of scare stories in the press.

One day, Pat was late coming into work. When he arrived, he looked pale.

"You all right, Pat?"

"Yes. Fine."

We knew each other well; I knew he wasn't fine. But he'd tell me in his own good time. At lunchtime, he took me for a drink.

"OK. What's wrong?" I asked as we sat in the garden of a local pub.

He looked at me, a strange look in his eyes.

"Craig's got AIDS." He was shaking. I didn't know what to say. I knew a little about his past. I knew he'd been as hedonistic as me, if not more. At least, until he'd met Craig.

"Oh, Pat," was all I could manage.

He looked directly at me. "I can already see him shrinking before my eyes, Mary."

"Is there nothing – "

"No. Nothing. He's going to die, Mary."

We sat quietly for a couple of minutes.

"How long?" I asked.

"Who knows? Nobody knows. But looking at the others, perhaps six months."

I knew I had to ask him the question.

"What about you?"

He flinched. "Did you have to ask?"

"Yes, Pat. I did. You're my best friend. I want to make sure you're all right."

"I got tested. I'm negative. For now."

"That's one good thing."

"Is it?" He asked, bitterness in his voice.

"Yes, Pat. What can we do for Craig?"

He shrugged. "Nothing. I've just got to look after him."

"What are you going to do?"

"I'll keep him at home as long as possible."

"Can I help?"

He looked at me. "You would, wouldn't you?"

"Yes, of course I would."

"No Mary. Thank you. But, no. God knows, there's enough stuff in the press about AIDS and most of it's crap. But I'm not letting you risk your life."

***

Over the next three months, Pat worked full time and looked after Craig as he faded away. I did visit him a couple of times, but we had never been close. What energy he had left was better used saying goodbye to others he knew better.

One weekend, Pat rang me to say Craig had been taken to hospital with pneumonia. We both knew what that meant in his weakened state. He died four days later.

Pat returned to work after a couple of weeks. I had read as much about AIDS as I could. Pat had been right. Most of the scare stories were idiotic. But widespread. I'd had a chat with Helena to explain everything I knew after she had queried if Pat was okay to still be working in the office.

He wasn't quite the same Pat. He'd lost friends already, but now he'd lost his partner. And I knew he felt the Sword of Damocles hanging over him; wondering if he was next.

***

A few months later, we were discussing something in the office. Nigel was on holiday. It was a dark day, and the lights were on; harsh fluorescent lights. I suddenly noticed lines on Pat's face that I hadn't noticed before. He looked gaunt. I must have stopped talking. He looked at me. In that moment, I knew. And he knew I knew. He slowly averted his eyes.

"How long ago, Pat?" I asked softly.

"Six weeks. Is it that obvious?"

"Only to someone who knows you well. Is there nothing they can do for you?"

"Only treat the symptoms. You saw what happened to Craig. It's my turn now."

"Are you feeling up to working?"

"At the moment. What else am I going to do? But I don't know how long for."

Not long at all, as it turned out. Only a few weeks later, he had deteriorated markedly. He lost weight at an alarming rate, and energy with it. One day, I took him home from the office early. He never returned. At his house, I realised he had been struggling more than he had let on. It was a mess. I set about clearing up. He tried several times to stop me. I sat him down.

"Pat, listen to me. You're my best friend. We've been through a lot over the years. If you think I'm going to just dump you here and leave you to it, think again."

"But the risks ..."

"I know the risks, Pat. I'm not an idiot. I've done my research, and I'm going to be careful. Now you sit there while I tidy this place up. Is there anything here you don't want me to find?"

He smiled briefly. "I don't think you'll find anything that'll shock you, Mary."

"Right. Do you have any gloves?"

We found some latex one's left over from Craig's time. I put them on and spent the next three hours tidying, cleaning, washing and organising.

I soon got into a routine. I went to work, then went to Pat's. I cooked for him when he wanted it. I did his washing and cleaning. He hated it at first. But eventually conceded that he couldn't do it himself. I persuaded him to contact his family. I wish I hadn't. He had finally told me that they had disowned him when he told them he was gay. The only reply he got was a note expressing surprise that his fate had taken so long.

The remaining members of the group were a lifeline as well, even though several had lost friends and lovers. They visited Pat, helped him, kept him in touch. But his decline was painful to watch. You could almost see it on a daily basis. His energy levels were low, his breathing poor. He could hardly move around the house.

One day, I was sitting by his bed. I'd filled him in on the day's events, as I always did. He was still Senior Clerk, after all. After a pause, he chuckled.

"Do you want to know something, Mary? I'm not frightened at all." He coughed weakly; his chest heavy. "Just waiting. Waiting for death."

I struggled to reply. I was fighting my tears. He saw.

"I'm going to have to leave you soon. No more holidays. No more gossip."

There was no point in denying it. We both knew it was true.

"Oh, Pat. I'm going to miss you so much." I couldn't hold back the tears. They streamed down my face.

"Promise me one thing, Mary."

"Anything, Pat."

"When I'm gone, get tested. Just to be sure."

"I will, I promise."

"And be careful in future. This isn't just about being gay, you know."

"I know Pat. I know."

One Friday night, two weeks later, Pat was taken into hospital with an infection. I spent hours sitting by his bed, but I wasn't there when he passed away on Sunday. I bitterly regret that.

I cried for days. He left a huge gap in my life. One that I struggled to fill for years.

Chapter 11 – Sacrifice

I did what many people do in the circumstances; I threw myself into my work. With Pat gone, I became Senior Clerk. Nigel was already self-sufficient, and we took on a new trainee. Ellen was very like me; she'd worked in a solicitor's office but wanted something better. She'd heard about this woman who had become a barrister's clerk, so wanted to follow her. It wasn't until she applied for the job that she found out she'd be working with me. She went on to prove her worth; many times over.

I didn't really have a social life for several months. I just didn't feel like it. But an event close to home made me value life that much more. I was visiting Catherine and the girls, and she happened to mention to me that she was going for an x-ray. When I asked why, she was a bit reticent, but eventually told me she'd found a lump in her breast. Since Mum had died of breast cancer, I'd been very careful to check myself regularly, and I had made Catherine promise she would too. But it was only this admission that proved to me she had been doing it.

"Do you want me to come with you?"

"Oh, no. I'm sure I'll be fine."

But she wasn't. She did have a lump. It turned out to be malignant. Given Mum's history, they decided to do a mastectomy, and then she had chemo and radiotherapy. All this took months, and I was surprised how resilient Catherine was. Of course, there was pain, and there were tears. It was hard; losing a breast and suffering all those side-effects.

But she never gave in. I must admit, I thought she might. And as after Mum's death, Tony came through for her. He was around for the time Catherine needed him. I spent quite a lot of time looking after the girls, but he always made sure that they and Catherine had the support they needed. He may not have been close to them, but he cared in his own way.

Sally was nine and had a fairly good idea of what was going on. Charlie was only five; she knew mummy was not very well, but not much beyond that. During the time I spent with them, I answered their questions as best I could. I struggled at times. I was a younger sister and didn't have children myself. Some of their questions were very direct, and I didn't know how honest to be in my answers. I think I got it about right.

After the courses of treatment ended, the doctors were optimistic. They gave her a clean bill of health; they could find no further traces of cancer. Our lives returned to a sort of normal. Tony disappeared again, Catherine became a full-time mum again, and I ... well, it was time to stop moping. It was time to enjoy life again.

The social club was the obvious place to start. I hadn't been to an event for months and started off with one of the evening get-togethers in a local pub. It was as if I'd never been away. I knew most of the people there, at least to some degree, and they welcomed me back. By the time I got home, I felt a lot more human.

Then I met the man who might have changed my life. Josh turned up to one of the groups meets. He was handsome, in a slightly shaggy way. Tall and slim, with shoulder-length blonde hair. A little ungainly, but a ready smile. At first, he appeared a bit arrogant, but I soon learnt that was something of an act. We chatted a couple of times, but it was mostly trivial stuff. Just being friendly. Then one week, for some reason, only about six of us turned up. Two couples, Josh, and me. Inevitably, we ended up talking most of the evening.

I heard his story; well, a lot of it. He was a year older than me but had packed a lot into that time. Backpacking around the world, a spell in the army, a variety of jobs. He'd been restless; searching for a role. Now he reckoned he'd found it. He worked for an overseas aid charity and positively loved it. As he talked about his work, there was an intensity to his voice and expression. At one point, he suddenly stopped.

"I'm sorry, Mary. I haven't shut up, have I? Typical man, I guess. Always talking about myself."

"Don't worry, Josh. You weren't really talking about yourself, anyway. It was your work that brought the passion out."

"Yea, I can tend to go off on one. Just tell me to shut up."

He asked about me; what I did, what I liked, was the group any good? I watched him as we talked. He appeared interested in what I said. Asked questions. Made me laugh. I couldn't remember when I had last laughed; really laughed.

"Why did you join the group, Josh?"

"I'm settled in my job now, for the first time in years. Well, the first time ever, really. I do travel quite a bit with work, but I thought it was time to give myself a base. The charity's HQ is here, so it seemed the obvious place to choose. But I don't know anyone, so felt I needed to get out a bit. You?"

"I joined a few years ago. All my contemporaries were getting married, having kids, settling down. I found myself at a bit of a loose end."

"Has it helped?"

I smiled. "Yes, everyone is really friendly. Lots of things going on. I've had some good times." A few vivid memories floated through my mind.

"You're not married then?"

"No. You?"

"No. I had to leave a relationship to move down here, but we hadn't been together long. It was amicable. She understood, at least."

"Didn't want to move down with you?"

"Couldn't really. Karen had family commitments that were important to her. I understood that, too."

"Sounds like two mature people making a sensible decision. You don't hear that much."

"Yea, I guess it was. I must have grown up."

"I know what you mean. I've had to do that a bit recently."

He raised an eyebrow. I told him about Mum, about Pat, about Catherine. He listened, not saying a word until I finished.

"Bummer," was all he said. We sat there in silence for a couple of minutes.

"Sorry," I said finally. "Didn't mean to bring it down."

"Oh, that's all right. It's these things that shape us. How about another drink?"

As he headed off to the bar, I realised the other two couples had gone. Looking at my watch, I found it was nearly closing time. We'd been talking longer than I thought. When he came back, we returned to lighter subjects. As we went to leave, he paused.

"Mary, do you fancy meeting up for a meal or something?"

"Yes, Josh. I do."

We met up a week later at a small restaurant I liked. For the first time in ages, I took time to get ready. Carefully choosing what to wear. A favourite set of underwear; all white, with little red details on the suspender belt. A dress that wasn't tight but followed my shape perfectly. And doing my hair and make-up a little less casually than normal.

By the time we'd settled at the table and ordered, I was as comfortable with Josh as I had at the pub.

"Where did you go backpacking?" I asked him.

"Oh, God. Where didn't I go? The Americas, almost from north to south. Australia, lots of Asian countries, and came back through Africa and Europe."

"How many times did you go?"

"Just the once. I was away for just over three years."

I looked up. "Wow, you didn't come home at all?"

"Nope."

"How old were you?"

"I left when I was nineteen."

"What did your mum and dad think?"

He paused, looking at me. I sensed I'd unintentionally intruded.

"Didn't have much to do with my family by then."

I knew not to probe further.

"How did you survive?"

"Quite easily, really. I set off with the basics and a bit of money. Then just did odd jobs when I needed money. Bars, shops, factories. Even taught a bit of English. I didn't need a lot. I ate cheaply and slept anywhere I could. In hostels, seedy hotels, outdoors if it was warm enough." He grinned. "And in girl's rooms."

"Lots of girls?"

He shrugged. "Yea. Lots of girls. I never said no, anyway."

"I'm guessing not many girls said no, either."

"Depends where you were, but I did all right. I was a bit of a lad. Never minded if a girl said no. Just tried someone else."

"So, what was your success rate?"

He frowned. "Don't know. I've never thought about it." I watched as he did some mental calculations. "About sixty per cent, I reckon."

"Amateur." He looked puzzled. "I can't remember any guy turning me down."

He relaxed, smiling. "I think women tend to be a bit more choosey than men."

"True. Although I probably wasn't when I was younger."

"Oh? Regrets?"

"Oh, no. I had a great time. But let's just say they weren't all equally memorable."

He smiled. "You speak as if that time is gone."

I swung a glass between my fingers. He was right.

"Yes, I suppose it is. I'm a bit old for all that now. It doesn't appeal anymore. And Pat's death was a warning as well. I realise I was lucky."

"I know that feeling. I think I was too. Considering where I travelled, and when. I got tested when I first met Karen."

"I did too. Pat made me promise. Were you okay?"

"Thankfully, yes. You?"

"Yes. But I breathed a huge sigh of relief."

We fell silent for a minute or two. I think we both knew that that exchange had been more significant than it sounded. We both knew how this evening was going to end and the feeling was strange. I was relaxed; comfortable; at ease. I knew he was coming home with me. I wanted him. But whereas previously, I'd have been like a girl on heat, desperate to leave and get on with the action, I felt as if there was no hurry. We had plenty of time. I wondered if I had finally grown up.

No. It wasn't that. I was no longer just looking for sex. Wanted it, yes. But I needed a guy I had some other connection with. More than purely physical. What I'd seen of Josh made me think he might fit the bill. We talked easily over the rest of the meal. We told each other about our lives and our dreams. All fairly light stuff; we didn't even flirt. Without debate, we agreed to split the bill.

"Shall we go?" I asked after we'd paid.

"I'm ready."

We walked out into the street, and I held out my hand to him. He took it, and I led him in the direction of my flat. Not much was said during the ten minutes it took to get home. I closed the front door behind us, and hung up my coat, taking his, and placing it next to mine. He stood waiting for me to lead through. But I walked over to him, placing my arms over his shoulders.

I pushed gently, until his back was against the wall, my arms wrapping around his neck. I placed my lips on his. His response was gentle and warm. It felt good; my need made itself known. His arms came around me, pulling me into him, until he was hugging me tightly, almost lifting me off the floor. One hand began to run down my back, and he slowly let it wander across my bum, following my curves.

It went lower, but he couldn't quite reach the hem of my dress. So, he started feeding material between his fingers to raise it. I pulled away from his kiss. I held out my hand again, and when he took it, I led him into the bedroom.

I released his hand and left him standing, while I put the bedside lights on. Walking back towards him, I stopped a few feet away. He watched me, silently, a slight smile on his face. I reached for the hem of my dress, and slowly lifted it until the whole thing came over my head, and I threw it over a chair. I followed his eyes, as they flowed over my body. I knew I looked good; he seemed to agree.

"Now," I said. "Where were we?" I moved forward until I was touching him. "Ah, I remember ..."

I took one of his arms, and put it around my back, and placed his other hand back on my bum. He laughed. I kissed him. His hands started to explore my body further, running lightly up and down my back, stroking my neck. He cupped my bum with both hands, and gently pulled me towards him. I felt his dick against my tummy.

"You're overdressed," I said and started to unbutton his shirt. He let me. Sliding my hands into the shoulders, the shirt fell to the floor. I knelt in front of him and undid his belt. Then the button and zip of his trousers, which slid down his legs. He lifted each foot in turn, and I pulled them clear, throwing them on the chair with my dress. I was facing a pair of black boxers with an interesting bulge in them. But still, there was no mad rush. I stood up, kissing him again. We both let our hands explore each other.

I slid my hands inside the back of his boxers and caressed his cheeks; tight and firm. He flexed them a couple of times, and I giggled. I let one hand come around the side, and finally reached his dick; hard and warm. A little hard breath caught in his throat as I did so. I used both hands to loosen his pants, pushed them over his hip, and they fell to the floor. He kicked them away. He moved his mouth to my ear.

"Now who's over-dressed?"

His hands went to the back of my bra and unhooked it. I freed my arms, so he could slip it off. He kissed me again, and with his hand on my shoulder, moved behind me. He put his hands on my tummy, and gently pulled me backwards. His dick pressed against my bum, and his hands started to caress my tummy, working up to my breasts. Gently stroking them he let his fingers play around my nipples. I just stood there, enjoying his touch. He was kissing the back of my neck; I always loved that. No hurry. No rush.

He let one hand slowly circle down my tummy, getting lower and lower, finally running over the top of my briefs. I wanted him to go lower still. He did. His fingers gently getting nearer and nearer. Finally, they touched my sex, and I flinched. He chuckled and withdrew, but I grabbed his hand and put it back.

This time, he covered me with his hand, gently sliding it between my legs. His fingers rubbing my pussy under the lace. His other hand was still caressing my breasts; his dick still pressing into my bum. It was about time I had a better look at it.

I slowly turned around and kissed him again. Then lowered myself to the floor. Face to face with his dick. Proudly standing, staring at me. I ran a hand up his thigh until it reached his balls and began massaging them with my fingers. I put my other hand on his hip, and slowly moved my mouth towards his dick. As I slid my lips over the head and moved down the shaft, he let out a long, low moan. I gently sucked on his dick, listening to the sounds this elicited. Those noises always turned me on, and I speeded up.

But he stopped me. Taking my arms, he raised me up again and began to kiss me. Lots of little, light kisses, all over my lips. Then, turning me, he led me to the bed and guided me onto it. He laid me on my back, and straddled me, his dick lying on my belly. I wrapped my arms around him, as we kissed. Then he began to move down me, slowly kissing my neck, then my shoulders, finally reaching my breasts.

Stroking and squeezing them with his hands, he took a nipple in his mouth. Sucking on it, teasing it with his teeth. Doing the same with the other. My hands played with his hair; long, silky. He moved one leg and pushed it between mine. I opened them, and he moved his other leg so that he was kneeling between them.

Moving down my abdomen, he kissed and caressed as he went. When he got to my briefs, he took the edge in his teeth, and looking up at me, playfully pulling on them. I giggled; he smiled. He sat up, and grabbed the briefs in both hands, sliding them off. I had to bring my legs up in front of him so that he could remove them. But then happily let them sink down either side of him again. He was looking down between my legs; smiling. That smile turned me on even more, and I spread my legs wider. Inviting his attention.

He looked up at me and placed a hand on each of my thighs. Still looking at me, he lowered himself and started to kiss my thighs, moving closer to my sex. As he reached my pussy, I let my head flop on the pillow and felt him gently sucking. The sensations flowed through me, as he played with my labia. Pulling them with his lips, licking them. I could feel his breath on my skin. He gently spread me wider with his fingers, as his tongue began to explore every fold.

Then he went for the bullseye. His tongue flicked my clit, and my body shuddered. He let it relax and then did it again. This time, he didn't stop. And he had me. I knew I was going to come; so did he. He kept up a steady, rhythmic movement, and moments later my orgasm pulsed through me. I let myself go; my breathing heavy and rapid. My legs shaking. He kept it up until I was about to stop him, but he didn't need to be told. He stopped and rested his head against my thigh. Letting me come down. No hurry. No rush.

After a while, I looked down at him. He was stroking my thigh, returning my gaze, and smiling. I went to move, but he stopped me and moved up over my body to kiss me. He reached out and grabbed a pillow. Kneeling up, he put it under my bum. Then he squatted between my legs and lifted my thighs over his.

I knew what he was going to do, and I wanted it. Shuffling forward, he laid his dick along my pussy. I put a hand down, and stroked it, pressing it onto me. He shifted slightly, and in one smooth move, slid himself into me. I'd only just come, but it felt so good.

Putting his arms under my knees, he began to rock backwards and forwards, moving my body at the same time. The two actions meant that his strokes were long and slow. He was watching me. Looking into my eyes, then looking down at my pussy as he slid in and out. My hand was still resting on my belly, and he picked it up and put it between my legs. I went for it. I closed my eyes. I could feel his dick stretching me with each movement. I could feel my own fingers on my clit. It didn't take long. As I came again, he pulled me firmly onto his dick, pausing with it deep inside me.

He held me there until my orgasm was over, gently relaxing his grip. I looked up at him again, watching me. That faint smile again. I let my breathing recover. Then decided it was time to take control. Sliding off his dick, I moved up the bed, leaving him in the same position. I knelt in front of him, giving him a few kisses, and then bent down.

His dick was glistening; covered in my juices. I grabbed it, and slowly licked it clean. Then taking more and more of him into my mouth each time, I began to move up and down. I could hear it was working. I put my hands around to grab his bum and took him as deep as I could, feeling his heat in my mouth.

I was going to finish him off, but he had other ideas. He gently pulled my head off. I looked up; he winked.

"Turn around."

I laughed. And eagerly complied. I got onto my hands and knees. Before I even found my balance, I gasped as his dick entered me, in one smooth, firm stroke. Without waiting, he started to fuck me. Deep, strong thrusts. Almost immediately, I knew I was going to come again.

I think it caught him by surprise this time, as I peaked. My hips must have bucked, because as I came, he grabbed them, and started to pound me. It was almost too much. I felt a bit light-headed. Suddenly, he cried out. He plunged deep into me and stayed there. His dick jerked. He resumed thrusting for a few more strokes as he came, grunting with each stroke. Then he slowed, sliding in and out a few more times.

I collapsed onto the bed, then squeaked as he collapsed on top of me, his dick being forced deep one more time.

"Sorry," he gasped, between rapid breaths.

"Okay," I replied, also trying to catch breath. "Just caught me by surprise."

He spread his legs either side of me to reduce his weight, and we lay there for several minutes. At some point, his dick popped out of me, causing us both to giggle.

"Shall I get something?" He asked.

"Nah. I can wash the bedding. You stay there. It feels good."

And it did. It was our first night together. The first of many. Over the next two years, we built a great relationship. Josh went abroad quite often. But never for more than a month at a time. When he was home, we spent a lot of time together. We clicked as people; we clicked as lovers.

We didn't make lots of plans for the future; we barely spoke about it. We enjoyed each other. But I think I loved him. I still don't really know. As all my friends had fallen in love, I wasn't even sure what that meant. I don't know why. Perhaps I'm odd.

But with Josh, it was different. We had common interests. Our sex life was almost perfect. And we were easy together. We never argued, never disappointed each other. Never demanded anything of each other; well, on occasion, but that was always fun. I felt good when he was around and missed him when he was away. If that was love, perhaps I'd finally found it.

Then fate intervened again. Catherine's cancer came back. With a vengeance. This time, nothing could be done. She was dead within six months of it being found. And I knew what I had to do. No, what I wanted to do.

Josh knew too. He knew me well by then. As Catherine declined, I spent more and more time helping Tony look after the girls. As before, he did all the practical stuff that was needed and did his best to support his wife. But I knew he wasn't ever going to be a stay-at-home father.

It wasn't discussed openly before Catherine died, although I'm sure they must have discussed it privately. She would have been worried sick about what would happen to the girls. Three days after the funeral, I sat Tony down. We had a long discussion. We argued, negotiated and came to an agreement.

Now I had to talk to Josh.

***

Looking back, that discussion was tough for both of us. Under different circumstances, I think Josh and I would have shared our lives. But it didn't happen. It wouldn't have worked in the circumstances. I had to put the girls first. I moved in with Sally and Charlie and looked after them for nearly five years. I gave up my lover. I gave up my career.

And now, I don't regret a minute of it. It was hard at times. I missed Josh. I missed work. But the chambers were brilliant; far better than I expected. They let me take six months off. Then I went back part-time. Not as Senior Clerk, of course. But they stood by me. As the girls became more settled, I increased my hours. When Tony installed Wendy in the house and she took over the girls, I moved out and went back full time. I was considerably richer by then, of course.

But those five years were the most rewarding of my life. And the biggest shock. I was a new parent with no time to learn. I suddenly had two girls of eleven and seven, who had just lost their mum. And their dad was absent most of the time. It was hard work, harder than I ever imagined. There were ups and downs; triumphs and disasters.

But when I see Sally now ...

See the woman she has become ...

It was all worth it.

Author's Note

I would like to thank all those involved in helping me bring this story to the page. You know who you are, and I will be eternally grateful.

If you haven't read Sally's Shadow, the first book in the Kinky Companions series, why not give it a go? Sally and Marcus (and Lucy) return in New Temptations, the second book in the Kinky Companions series. Mary features in the story, as always. I hope you'll join them in their adventures.

To keep in touch with my writing, you can visit my website, where you can subscribe to my newsletter or blog, or follow me on social media.

Website: www.alexmarkson.com
Twitter: @amarksonerotica
Facebook: Alex Markson
Goodreads: Alex Markson

Alex Markson
February 2020

Printed in Great Britain
by Amazon

26468811R00098